Before I Knew

CARRIE ANN RYAN

I0594096

Before I Knew

A CAGE FAMILY PREQUEL

SPECIAL EDITION

CARRIE ANN RYAN

Before I Knew

Before I Knew
A Cage Family Prequel
By: Carrie Ann Ryan
© 2024 Carrie Ann Ryan

Cover Art by Wildfire Designs

For the ones who never gave up.
And the ones still trying their best.

Praise for Carrie Ann Ryan

"Count on Carrie Ann Ryan for emotional, sexy, character driven stories that capture your heart!" – Carly Phillips, NY Times bestselling author

"Carrie Ann Ryan's romances are my newest addiction! The emotion in her books captures me from the very beginning. The hope and healing hold me close until the end. These love stories will simply sweep you away." ~ NYT Bestselling Author Deveny Perry

"Carrie Ann Ryan writes the perfect balance of sweet and heat ensuring every story feeds the soul." - Audrey Carlan, #1 New York Times Bestselling Author

"Carrie Ann Ryan never fails to draw readers in with passion, raw sensuality, and characters that pop off the page. Any book by Carrie Ann is an absolute treat." – New York Times Bestselling Author J. Kenner

"Carrie Ann Ryan knows how to pull your heartstrings and make your pulse pound! Her wonderful Redwood Pack series will draw you in and keep you reading long into the night. I can't wait to see what comes next with the new generation, the Talons. Keep them coming, Carrie Ann!" – Lara Adrian, New York Times bestselling author of CRAVE THE NIGHT

"With snarky humor, sizzling love scenes, and brilliant, imaginative worldbuilding, The Dante's Circle series reads as if Carrie Ann Ryan peeked at my personal wish list!" – NYT Bestselling Author, Larissa Ione

"Carrie Ann Ryan writes sexy shifters in a world full of passionate happily-ever-afters." – *New York Times* Bestselling Author Vivian Arend

"Carrie Ann's books are sexy with characters you can't help but love from page one. They are heat and heart blended to perfection." *New York Times* Bestselling Author Jayne Rylon

Carrie Ann Ryan's books are wickedly funny and deliciously hot, with plenty of twists to keep you guessing. They'll keep you up all night!" USA Today Bestselling Author Cari Quinn

"Once again, Carrie Ann Ryan knocks the Dante's Circle series out of the park. The queen of hot, sexy, enthralling paranormal romance, Carrie Ann is an author not to miss!" *New York Times* bestselling Author Marie Harte

Before I Knew

It all began with a wrong number.

When Blakely gets added to the Cage family group chat, chaos ensues. What she doesn't expect is to have a side chat with the eldest brother.

What was supposed to be a simple sign off, turns into a mild flirtation and invitation to lunch.

Only Aston Cage has his secrets.

And perhaps they should've left their conversation on read.

Before I Knew is the prequel to the Cage family series. Learn how Blakely and Aston met, before they finally get their happily ever after in The Forever Rule.

Chapter 1
Aston

Wait. Why did we make a group chat? I thought we already had a group chat? One with a name and everything.

FLYNN:

We had to make a new one because somebody ruined the last one.

DORIAN:

I feel like there was a little sarcasm in your pointed tone.

HUDSON:

How do you hear tone in a text message?

THEO:

Oh, we read tone.

FORD:

Seriously though, why the new group chat? Do you understand how many group chats I have?

FLYNN:

It's not our fault that you decided to marry two people who had large families.

HUDSON:

Greer's is a large family with three brothers and a bunch of spouses. Noah's family? Calling the Montgomerys large is like saying the earth is part of the solar system.

DORIAN:

That wasn't even a good analogy. You should have said something like water is wet.

THEO:

Oh, so are we making fun of Hudson's bad analogy here? Because I'm here for it.

ME:

I still want to know why we have a new group chat. Why we're even starting with the group chat.

FLYNN:

Because Dorian added his ex to the previous group chat, and I didn't know how to quietly remove her without notifying her.

ME:

Are you serious? She was in there the whole time.

HUDSON:

You don't just add someone to the group chat. You make a separate group chat.

THEO:

That's the whole rule of group chats. What is said in group chat, stays in group chat.

HUDSON:

Until you take a screenshot of your chat and then you put it in the other chat hoping that the person that you're talking shit about doesn't actually see it. And now I've confused myself.

ME:

I hate all of you.

FORD:

You love us. Seriously though, do not add spouses to the family group chat. Or parents. We have a family group chat with the parents, and then a family group chat with just Mom, and then one with just Dad. Hence why I'm very confused why we continue to have more of them. We need to name this one.

ME:

Let's just call it the Cages.

FLYNN:

Yes, because we don't have anything called the Cages in the Cage family group chat. You're the CEO of this family, what the hell's wrong with you?

HUDSON:

He's the president of Cage Enterprises. Not the CEO of the family.

FLYNN:

For a man that doesn't work with the company, you do sound a little testy.

DORIAN:

Those sound like fighting words to me.

JAMES:

I have been in a meeting this entire time. Are we seriously just going to have a fifty-message long group chat about the efficacies and rules of group chat? This isn't Fight Club.

THEO:

All the more reason to actually speak about the group chat, as we're allowed to talk about it. Like you said, this isn't Fight Club.

FORD:

I thought we weren't supposed to talk about fight club.

HUDSON:

That movie came out what, fifty years ago at this point?

FLYNN:

Let's not let Hudson do math anymore.

ME:

Seriously. Now that we know we have a new group chat, we can come up with a name later.

FLYNN:

Fine by me. Did you start this discourse for a reason, eldest brother of ours?

ME:

I wanted to ensure we were all ready for family dinner on Friday. You know, our favorite thing to do.

HUDSON:

Groan.

DORIAN:

I'm busy.

JAMES:

New phone, who's this?

THEO:

Yes, because that totally works, James. Wait. Does it work? I need to know. For reasons.

FORD:

I will probably have dinner with the Montgomerys. In fact, I'll make sure I'll have dinner with the Montgomerys.

ME:

Dad won't be there. He's on a work trip.

THEO:

I'm in.

HUDSON:

Friday night at six again?

DORIAN:

I might not make it until six thirty.

JAMES:

I'll be there. We can hitch a ride together, Flynn.

FLYNN:

What if I have a date?

DORIAN:

You guys, I can't laugh so hard that I pee myself in public. Flynn. A date.

FLYNN:

Your urinary tract problems aren't my problems.

FORD:

I might have a Montgomery dinner, but I'm going to try to make it.

ME:

Dinner is at seven. Drinks begin at six. I suppose it's my turn to host. Unless we'd like to go to The Teal Door?

THEO:

Do not ruin my restaurant with a family dinner that will surely be loud and rowdy.

JAMES:

We are elite businessmen. We are not rowdy.

DORIAN:

I'd rather go to the restaurant.

THEO:

You are not allowed to date any more of my waitresses. One quit already.

ME:

Dorian, what the hell did you do?

DORIAN:

I didn't do anything. Laura said she was moving to be near her mom because she got sick. I may like women, but I don't fuck with them.

HUDSON:

Sure, Dorian. Whatever you say.

DORIAN:

I'm offended.

THEO:

You really aren't.

JAMES:

You really, really aren't.

ME:

We'll pick the place soon. But Theo, is it okay if we use your place instead? I'd rather not have to deal with a caterer. I could cook, but I don't have time.

THEO:

Fine. However, just know I'm going to charge you out the ass.

ME:

Charge the company.

DORIAN:

Wait, you're not even going to cook for us, Aston?

ME:

I'm not in the mood to search for a middle finger emoji.

FLYNN:

My God, how old are you?

JAMES:

We don't ask those types of questions.

UNKNOWN NUMBER:

Hello? Do you know how to exit a group chat? Not that this hasn't been enlightening, but I don't think I'm supposed to be here.

I LEANED BACK AND STARED AT MY PHONE AS IF IT were a snake ready to strike. I did not recognize the number. It wasn't Dorian's ex. And now I was wondering why we had a complete stranger in our family group chat. Damn it. I picked up the phone as soon as it rang, Flynn's name appearing on the screen.

"Do you know who that is?" Flynn asked, his voice sounding slightly panicked.

"Is it weird that I hope it's someone that Dorian met and accidentally put her number in?" Because having it be a complete stranger would be worse. At least we hadn't shared company and family issues within the chat. So far.

"We don't know if it's a *her*."

That was true. We didn't know if it was a <u>her</u>. And here I was, acting as if it could be. Weird.

"Hell, no one else is texting, so they're probably waiting for me to handle it?" I ask, pinching the bridge of my nose.

"Sounds about right. But you are the big brother. It's what you're used to. Handle it."

"At least we didn't discuss company secrets."

"No, we just said our names often enough that now someone has our numbers. Hopefully it's not the press. Or a rival. Fuck."

I could practically see Flynn pace his office. We weren't working in the same building today. Flynn was off in the small town that we had purchased over two generations ago, while I was in our high-rise in the city of Denver. I liked running Cage Enterprises. Our grandfather, and later our father, had built it from the ground up, and while they had made some questionable business choices along the way, we had changed the game. We worked with gaining financing and worked with ethical and environmentally friendly building. Hence why we worked with Ford's family, the Montgomerys so often. We worked with real estate development, small business backers, and environmental research. Meaning we had way too many NDAs to begin with, and people were constantly trying to reach us.

And now, we were adding random people to group chats.

Again, the group chat went completely silent, and I copied the person's number before starting a new chat.

ME:

> Sorry about that. Wrong number I assume?

The three little dots flared for a moment, before they went away, and I had to hope that that was for the best.

UNKNOWN NUMBER:

> I wouldn't know. You're the one now texting me outside the group chat. Where did you get my number?

I studied the number, then quickly went through my contacts, and cursed under my breath. It was one away from Dorian's. Meaning, when Flynn had made the group chat, he had somehow typed in Dorian's number. Which didn't make any sense to me because you could just go through the contact list. I quickly called up Flynn again.

"How did you make the group chat?"

"My phone was giving me problems, so I just typed in everyone's numbers. I have them all memorized."

I rolled my eyes. "Of course you do. But you added one more you shouldn't have."

Flynn cursed under his breath. "Apparently I was tired."

"Apparently I have to clean up your messes."

"It's a chat. We'll delete it. Breathe."

I rolled my eyes at the fact that it was Flynn telling me to calm down now. That was rich. "You were the one panicking before. Because now this person has our numbers, our names, and where we'll be on Friday."

"Yes. Because she could be a sniper. We've just alerted our own demise where we'll be. It'll make it easy for them. But hopefully I'll have wine beforehand."

"I hate when you get all quick-witted after you're done panicking because you know I'll handle it."

"It's like you know me. Got to go. Meeting's starting."

I sighed, then gestured for James to come in as he walked across my office and set down a stack of papers. He raised a brow, and I sighed, gesturing toward the phone.

"I'll handle it."

"It's not anything to handle. But I'll see you soon."

"Yeah. You will."

I liked the fact that James and Flynn worked with me. I didn't feel like I was constantly searching to find my large family. I had way too many brothers to count. Okay, I had six brothers. With Flynn and Hudson as twins, Ford was the youngest, and I was the oldest. And yet Ford was the one who was married and happy and settling in his life. The rest of us were figuring out what we wanted. That was fine though, it wasn't as if my end of days were here. But I was busy with work, far too busy to deal with something like a relationship. Flynn and James worked hours just as long as I did.

And I knew Theo as a chef and a restaurant owner worked off hours, to the point that we rarely got to see him. Dorian was on the same hours as Theo since he owned a bar and grill that went for high class clientele even though the place was called The Cage of all things. I rolled my eyes at that.

Hudson and Ford were the only two that really didn't work for the company anymore. With Ford working for a security company that he owned with his spouse and his spouse's family, and Hudson painting for a living. It was odd to think that there was even an artist in our family, since it wasn't something that our father had really subscribed to. But Hudson had always gone his own way. After all, he had done his stint in the Army, spending far too many years overseas where we couldn't get ahold of him.

But now we were all here, doing something as casual as family dinner.

And apparently had just invited this stranger.

ME:

We're sorry for bothering you. You can just remove yourself from the group chat by hitting the information button.

UNKNOWN NUMBER:

Hmph. I should have thought of that. Sorry it's been a long day. But you guys sound hilarious. Brothers I take it?

I frowned, wondering why this person wanted the information, and why I wanted to answer.

ME:

Yes. Should I ask your name since you know mine?

UNKNOWN NUMBER:

You say that as if I could figure out who was who from the texts. There were a lot of them.

My lips curled into a smile.

ME:

Hazard a guess.

UNKNOWN:

I'm afraid to. But I assume you're the eldest from the way you're trying to take care of everything and texted me outside of the chat.

I frowned, wondering how this person could know this.

That was a little too intuitive and it made me uncomfortable.

ME:

And what's your name?

ME:

It seems only fair to ask.

UNKNOWN NUMBER:

Well, since you haven't asked for my location yet, I guess I can't be too worried about you being a serial killer.

ME:

I feel like I should be the one worried.

UNKNOWN NUMBER:

Blakely. My name's Blakely.

ME:

Well, Blakely. It is nice to meet you.

BLAKELY:

Nice to meet you as well. Although this isn't how I usually talk to men on phones or even on the internet. I don't like things like that. In fact, I should probably put my phone down before I realize you're a scam.

My lips twitch, and I did the one thing I should have done this whole time, I Googled the number.

And because the internet always showed everyone's secrets unless you knew how to hide them, I found it far too easily.

Blakely Graves.

I didn't look beyond the first page, but I wanted to make sure that she wasn't a scammer or anything.

But Blakely Graves was a real person. And the photo attached to her profile that came from a job search site made my breath catch.

Gorgeous light eyes, blonde waves falling past her shoulders. And hell. Now I felt like the stalker here. Maybe I was the one asking for too much.

ME:

> Anyway, I have to get back to work. But sorry for interrupting your day.

BLAKELY:

> I've had a long and tedious day. So thanks for making me laugh. And you should totally cook for them. Not just do catering. At least one time.

I rolled my eyes.

ME:

> Did you see how many of them there are? No thanks. Plus I don't want to poison them.

BLAKELY:

> Good to know. Have a good day and I'll remove myself.

I looked at the chat and saw the notification that she had indeed removed herself from the chat. I didn't know why I felt a little sad about it. But I ignored it, and ignored the rest of the group chat as the brothers continued to talk now that they felt a bit safer after she left. Instead, I went back to work, my gaze looking at my phone every once in a while.

I didn't want her to text back. I didn't even know this person. I was just a little too tired.

I had been working too many long hours and knew the chaos was because I was trying to clean up a few messes my father had set to the side when he'd decided to retire. He was good at that. Making big promises and working on a few of them so they shone, and then letting everything else fall by the wayside. And I cleaned them up. Along with Flynn and the others, but it was mostly me.

And it wasn't as if Mom wanted anything to do with the company, or anything that came along with owning the town.

Because the Cages didn't just work in down-towns and across the world in high rises. No, we owned a whole town.

One in the mountains of Colorado, that was just for the Cages.

I had always thought as a child it was fun to have a town named after us, the one that held our legacy.

I just hadn't realized how much paperwork came with such an accolade.

Because we were not small town people. At least I didn't think so. My brothers on the other hand, they fit in a little bit more. Me though? I needed my suit and tie and martini. I wanted my Mercedes, and not the off-roader. I didn't want to deal with snow where we also had to be the ones who plowed.

I had too many other things on my mind.

Didn't that make me sound like a pompous ass.

I picked up my phone again, knowing I was distracted.

ME:

So do you think it's going to snow tomorrow?

I set down the phone again, wondering why I was even asking. It was ridiculous. But I couldn't get those eyes out of my head.

BLAKELY:

Probably. And then it'll be eighty degrees by the end of the day. It's Colorado. It's how we do weather.

ME:

So are you from here then?

I paused, wondering how to word it.

ME:

> You have a Colorado number, so I just assumed you were local. But that doesn't mean anything anymore because we all have cell phones all over the world.

BLAKELY:

> As soon as I typed my response, I realized the same thing. I don't even know why I replied.

BLAKELY:

> But no, I'm from here. Born and bred. I wouldn't know where west is if I left. I need the mountains.

As the Rocky Mountains in Denver were always on the west, you always knew where north was. It did help with directions.

ME:

> I got lost when I was in Central Pennsylvania once. We were in a valley, and I couldn't figure out where north was. It didn't help that it was overcast, and I couldn't see the sun.

BLAKELY:

> You know our phones have compasses on them. And GPS.

ME:

> Yes, but I couldn't look down when I was driving. And I couldn't figure out the rental car. It was a thing.

Now I felt embarrassed, like an idiot for even saying anything. I ran a multi-million-dollar corporation and several businesses, and I couldn't figure out a rental car. Or at least that one day had been a nightmare. I never showed weakness. That's how people took advantage of you. But apparently it was easy to do so over a single chat where neither of you knew the other in real life.

BLAKELY:

> No it's okay. I'm the same way. I have to get into a meeting though, okay? Talk to you later?

BLAKELY:

> Or not. Since we're strangers.

I smiled then, typing right back.

ME:

> Talk to you later.

But we didn't, at least not that night. The next morning I was working, dealing with a thousand meetings and papers on my desk, and when the snow began to fall in earnest, I smiled and picked up my phone.

ME:

Well, it is indeed snowing.

BLAKELY:

Good thing I dressed in layers. I wonder what the weather will be like later today.

A few hours later, my phone buzzed.

BLAKELY:

It is 75 degrees outside. I do not understand this weather.

A few days later, I picked up the phone again when it buzzed.

BLAKELY:

Did you see that score last night?

ME:

Only a few glimpses of it. I didn't see the last save.

BLAKELY:

The Avs are my team for a reason.

ME:

Well, brand loyalty helps. Although I used to be a Penguins fan as well.

BLAKELY:

I can't believe you just said that. I think I'm going to have to delete your number.

ME:

That would be a horrible reason for you to do that.

BLAKELY:

Okay true. But tell me you're at least a Broncos fan.

ME:

I can neither confirm nor deny. But I do like going to the games.

We had box seats for the Avs as well, but I only got to go to those when we had to bring in partners and clients. I rarely got to enjoy myself with things like going to games and having fun. Maybe I did need a weekend out in the town. Cage Lake had a little inn where you could rest and relax—though Flynn was the only one of us who had stayed there as of yet. The Cages owned the resort and many of the buildings in town, but we didn't tend to live there. We each had homes along the lake though, so I could just head there. Though I knew Flynn was renting his out right now.

Maybe I needed a break. Maybe I needed to go to a game.

The next day, I was the one who texted first.

ME:

Did you see that game?

BLAKELY:

No I missed it. Deadline.

I didn't know what she did for a living, nor was I sure she knew that I was Aston Cage. It wasn't that I was famous or anything, but in certain circles, people knew who our family was. That's why we were always careful about who we let in. Dorian may have played around, but he was still damn careful.

Hence why a group chat could change things.

ME:

It was a good game. I wish I could have gone.

BLAKELY:

Maybe someday.

The next day I texted again.

ME:

Let's meet for coffee.

I hadn't even realized I was typing it until the bubble exclaimed it was sent and there was no going back.

I just wanted to know who this woman was. I could have Googled more. I could have asked someone to look into her. The information was at my fingertips. But I couldn't get past my curiosity about the woman who made me laugh with just a few text messages.

BLAKELY:

I'm still not sure you're not a serial killer.

I grinned, grateful she was at least a little cautious. I sure as hell wasn't right then.

ME:

Public place and all. I promise I won't take you to a secondary location.

I wasn't sure if that sounded creepy or like a come on, but when she gave me a laughing emoji, my shoulders relaxed.

BLAKELY:

I shouldn't.

ME:

We should do it anyway.

BLAKELY:

Okay, that sounds like a good
argument.

I straightened in my chair, my hand tightening around my phone.

ME:

Okay then. Tomorrow? Just coffee.
No murder.

BLAKELY:

Okay. I can do that. Not the murder
thing. Although all I know about you
is that you live in Colorado. You
could be hours away.

ME:

Meet me at Taboo. Do you know
that place? It's downtown.

I could see the chat bubble light up again before she answered.

BLAKELY:

I know the place. And I work
downtown. Coincidence.

Yeah, coincidence. Or maybe *she* was a serial

killer.

I had a date with a wrong number.

And I didn't want to be wrong about *this*.

Chapter 2
Blakely

"I'M DEFINITELY GOING TO BE MURDERED, right?" I asked as I paced my bedroom.

My best friend Isabella stared at her phone while perched on the edge of my bed, her legs crossed, and a small frown on her face.

When she didn't say anything, I cleared my throat and asked again. "Am I really going to get murdered if I do this?"

Isabella put down her phone and looked up at me, a small smile playing on her face now. I had known Isabella for years and she was one of my best friends. She was also one of the most beautiful people I knew. Her whole family was, if I were honest. She had three gorgeous sisters, and her brother was a man who apparently made people swoon when he walked into a room. I had always thought of him as Isabella's younger brother, so that hadn't been a thing in my eyes. But now as I stared at my friend, I had to wonder if I'd lost my mind about the decisions I'd made.

"No. Maybe. I hope not."

"Not helpful." We grinned at each other before she shook her head.

"Honestly, a group chat? So they just entered your number and suddenly you were part of their meeting? That sounds a little suspicious."

"I know, right? But it does happen. You've heard of it happening. There was that whole viral moment where a grandma texted the wrong person inviting him to Thanksgiving, and then it turned into this heartwarming thing."

"I remember that. It's just all that had happened with a group chat. You usually have to add contacts."

"Maybe he typed it in. Who knows. But I was in there, and all of the people sounded like they were joking around and they were a family who cared about each other. A real family with sarcasm as their love language."

"And so the real family is why you're going to go on this coffee date?"

I ran my hands down my dove-gray slacks, and immediately went to take them off, knowing I needed to wear something different. Maybe a skirt. Yes, a skirt would be good.

"Are you getting naked for me for a reason?" Isabella asked, and I flipped her off before putting my pants back on. "I was thinking about wearing a skirt, but then that seemed a little too forward."

"You mean one of your A-line pencil skirts? No, that wouldn't be too forward. And we're going to be late and hit every ounce of rush hour if you don't make a decision. You look gorgeous, Blakely. Live in it. Be in it."

I held back a smile since she sounded like the trainer in the classic *Miss Congeniality*. "Thank you for coming over. I know you're busy and you don't have time to deal with my insecurities and the fact that I'm going on a blind date with a man I'm randomly texting about the weather and Avalanche games."

"I still can't believe he said he was a Penguins fan." Isabella held up her hand. "It's okay. We all have a thing for Crosby."

I gave her a wry smile as I met her reflection in

the mirror. "I'm sure there are other guys on the team you know."

My best friend shrugged. "Well, I don't really pay attention to them unless they are my team. It's not like I have time."

"You work more hours than I do."

"Maybe. But it's what I do. It's life. Now, you look wonderful, for work, and for a simple coffee. I like Taboo. They have great sandwiches, and I go in for a different type of coffee every time. They seem to fit my moods. It's a little creepy actually."

"I'm going to a creepy coffee place to go meet a serial killer," I blurted, and Isabella let out a deep breath, calming herself while I did the same. She knew I was on a downward spiral, and I needed to lift myself out of it if there was any way for me to make it through the day.

"You've been to Taboo. You like their coffee. You also like the look of the very hot tattoo artist next door."

I bit my lip and inhaled before letting out a long breath. "That is true. And there's a bookstore that I love nearby. In fact, I love that whole street. It's like a little oasis in the middle of downtown. This is fine. It's just coffee. It's a public space."

"Do you know his name?" she asked.

I froze, realizing that I didn't. That seemed like a little oversight and yet I knew it was for a reason. Being strangers in a text chain was easier to lean into than knowing who this man was. However I was about to meet him. "I don't. I don't even know what he looks like. I'm just going to meet some guy holding a phone in a coffee shop. I could sit next to anyone. This is so unlike me."

"Just Google his phone number and figure out who it is." Isabella reached for my phone, and I snatched it back, feeling a little protective of it. When she raised her brows, I winced.

"I don't know if I want to know."

"What are you worried about? That he is married? Someone you know? A ninety-year-old man?"

I put my face in my hand and groaned. "This is ridiculous. I should just look up his number."

"You should have done it weeks ago."

However, I did what I should and typed the number into my search engine.

"Do you really have it memorized?" Isabelle asked and I tried to ignore the humor in her tone.

I didn't look at her face, my cheeks burning. "We've been talking. It's been nice. And I've been looking at the number instead of a name because I couldn't add him to my contacts."

Yet everything changed with a single page load on my browser. I shouldn't have been surprised that the world was a little ironic. Because as soon as the page loaded, I stood in my room, mouth agape as Isabella sucked in a breath.

"Aston Cage?" I blurted, my voice going high-pitched. "Aston Cage. Of the Cage family? *Cage Enterprises*?"

"Your voice is getting a little high-pitched."

My hands gripped my phone so tightly, my knuckles went white. "It should be. Aston Cage. I know this man."

Isabella's eyes shot up to mine. "You've met him before?"

I shook my head. "No, my boss just hates him. Because a lot of times we go for the same developments, and they win."

"Because the Cages are a little savvier than your boss. You know that. That's why you work for your boss. You're always fixing everything he messes up."

I held up my hand. "I don't have time to worry too much about that. But look at him. *Look at him.*" I held up my phone to her and waved it around.

"What am I supposed to be looking at? He looks

like a dude. With hair. That seems to be a little dark. Sometimes he has a beard in these photos, sometimes not. And he looks to do a lot of galas. That sounds boring."

I turned the phone back to me, and scrolled, realizing that he was indeed on the arm of a different woman in practically each one. Gorgeous statuesque women and variety of color of dresses. All for galas. "Oh, this is so stupid. This is Aston Cage. That means I was in the group chat of the *Cage family*."

"They aren't gods. Though your boss would've loved that."

My gaze shot to hers. "He can never find out. No wonder they all ghosted the chat right before I left. They had to be freaking out."

"It's not like they're going to divulge family and business secrets in a group chat. At least I would hope not. They seem smarter than that."

"But it's *Aston Cage*."

"Is he a playboy or something? I'm an accountant. I don't know these things," Isabella said with a sigh.

"You're a brilliant accountant, and no, I don't think so. Maybe. That doesn't matter. He's gorgeous."

"He's a man."

I laughed at that, shaking my head. "Maybe you're the one who needs to go out and meet somebody."

"The next time I get added to a family group chat, maybe I will. But I have enough in my life to deal with. Especially because we're going to be late. Now go to this coffee thing. Let one of us live a little. You're going to be fine."

"I can't believe you of all people are the one pushing me into this."

"I'm living vicariously through you. Your job is more fun, your life is more fun, and you're going to meet a CEO who could take over the world. I don't see the problem here."

"I see a very big problem here."

"What's the worst that can happen?" she asked, sounding so much unlike Isabella, I was afraid we had somehow switched places.

"Are you kidding me right now?"

"I have your phone tracked, and I'll put an AirTag on you. I'll know where you are at all times."

"That sounds a little more like the real Isabella," I said with a laugh, as I hugged her tightly. She patted my back, and then pushed off me.

"Now let's go. I'm not in the mood to deal with assholes on the highway. Which is every day."

"Thank you for getting here before the sun even rose."

"It's because I love you. And I needed to make sure that our tracking is going well."

I laughed at her, and we made our way to our respective jobs, that tension writing the back of my mind the entire time.

Work seemed to go at a slog all day. I enjoyed my job. I enjoyed strengthening businesses and figuring out which player was best for which position, but my boss of Howard Enterprises didn't play well with my ideas. But it was my job to make sure that we didn't go under and break the rules.

I wasn't a CEO. I wasn't a CFO. I was someone who had to have my hands in a thousand pots at once. And I enjoyed it. That meant I had to keep my mind on task, and I wasn't doing it very well because I was sitting here wondering what the hell I was going to do.

"Blakely, do you have the report?" Mr. Howard said from my doorway, and I smiled at him. The man didn't specify which report and could have just emailed me. He didn't have to walk across the office just to ask me about a report that was probably already in his inbox and printed out in triplicate because that's how he liked things. Who needed to save trees?

"Which report?" I asked.

He scowled at me, and I knew that was probably the wrong thing to say. "You know, the report. The one I've been waiting on."

"It should be in your inbox." Again, I had no idea what report he was talking about, because *he* didn't know what report he was talking about, but I was up to date on what he needed from me, so it would be in his inbox. His team of assistants should have already handled it, but he liked to look grumpy and in charge on the floor. It lent a sense of control that I didn't understand, but he said it worked.

I had to remind myself I really loved my job when people did what they were supposed to do. Even though it wasn't my biggest fan right now.

"Good, good. You're still on for the gala this weekend?"

"I'll be there. It's a lovely charity event."

"Yes, but we have to make sure we don't let the Cages outshine us. You know them. They always like to walk around like little peacocks, pluming their little feathers."

I wasn't even sure that was true, but I did my

best to keep a straight face. Because I was about to go on a coffee date with the head peacock.

Oh, God. This was such a bad idea.

"I will do my best to not let them take over."

"Good. It's a charity event, and we need to make a stand."

It was a charity event and that meant we should probably give to charity and raise awareness, but sure, making a stand worked. With that, Mr. Howard stomped off, probably to go growl at someone else, and I looked down at my phone, and realized I had fifteen minutes to get to Taboo. I quickly set everything as idle, nodded at my assistant, and made my way down the high-rise.

I loved living in Denver, I loved the view, the air. I even loved the insane weather that never made any sense. I lived in a suburb like most people who drove into the city, not downtown, but I didn't even mind the commute. When I had lived on the east side of town, I had been able to take the light rail in, but the west side of town didn't have everything I needed yet. But they were working on it, *so they said*.

I let out a deep breath. I spent so much time these days trying to live in my head rather than in the reality of the job I hated. So focusing on the commute and my family meant I didn't dwell on the day-to-day life that was slowly sucking the life from me.

Everything was fine. I loved this.

I loved my job.

The fact that I kept having to say that worried me, but it was a dream job. I sort of made it up as I went along and excelled in a business that stressed me out—when they powers that be allowed me.

And now I was meeting with my boss's rival. This was going to go lovely.

But he didn't know who I was. Unless he googled my number like I should have done this whole time. That seemed like a very big lapse in judgment.

I walked the two blocks toward the center of town, and finally made my way to the main street that I loved. There were little cafés and small businesses everywhere. Nothing looked too commercialized or downtrodden. People seemed to like each other on this particular street. It was always surprising since most of the time people tended to ignore each other.

Taboo had been located here since before I started working, and probably years before that. I loved the coffee and the pastries and needed to come down here for sandwiches more often, but I ate at my desk more than I should.

I looked down at my gray pants and soft pink top, and realized I looked like a business professional, not someone off to get afternoon coffee with a man I didn't even know.

Except for the fact I knew his name and what he looked like.

This was insane.

"Get over it, Blakely. It's a cup of coffee," I muttered to myself before opening the door to walk in.

There could have been tables around or even cute decorations. There could have been a thousand people in there, begging for coffee and pastries, but I didn't see them.

Instead, I only saw him.

Aston Cage.

All six-foot-something of him in a dark gray suit that fit him to a tee. Clearly bespoke or tailored perfectly for him. His piercing blue eyes caught me in a web, and I couldn't stop looking at him.

He was built, broad shouldered, but it narrowed down at the waist, so almost like a swimmer's body. His hair was dark, longer on the top than the sides, and perfectly coiffed as if he spent far too long in the mirror.

Or maybe he just woke up like that. Perfect and amazing.

Somebody bumped into me, and I moved to the side, realizing that I was blocking the door.

"I'm sorry."

"It's okay. If I had someone looking at me like that, I'd stand there too," the stranger said before she waved her fingers at me and him and moved back.

I moved to the side then, as Aston came forward.

"Hi," I whispered.

"Hi," he said right back, his voice deep, intoxicating.

What was with this? We hadn't even said anything.

When his lips quirked into a smile, I blinked, telling myself to snap out of it.

"I see you also Googled me," he said softly.

"I'm sorry. Hi, I'm Blakely," I said, awkwardly holding out my hand.

Aston looked down at it, that smile still on his face, and slid his hand over mine. "Aston. Can I get you a cup of coffee?"

"That would be lovely," I said with a laugh, and

then he did the silliest and most attractive thing ever, and lifted my hand to his lips, and I knew there was a problem.

"Oh wow," another woman said as she walked by, fanning herself.

I blushed and took my hand back. "Now that I'm done making a scene. I'd love coffee. Though I am more of a latte girl."

"We can do a latte."

"Should I ask if you do this often? I feel like I should ask if you do this often."

"I have never asked a wrong number out for coffee before. Though I have been here before. Not with another woman though."

"Oh. That's good."

"It is."

We ordered our coffees, talking of weather and sports like we were good at, and I had to wonder if we would talk about anything else.

But it was just coffee after all.

The place was full, so we ended up sitting outside at a little table, nerves running through me.

"So. I would ask what you do, but I sort of know what you do."

"My brother who works in security would probably want to know if you knew that before you Googled me."

I blinked. "As in I somehow entered myself into your life through a random text message? Like I'm the one who typed it in?"

"That's what he would want to know. I assumed that you didn't somehow secretly break into my other brother's house to type in your phone number."

My lips quirked, my shoulders immediately relaxing.

"Yes, it was all an accident. And I actually didn't Google your name until this morning."

Heat crossed my cheeks, and Aston leaned back and blinked at me. "Really? So you didn't know my name this whole time?"

"It was an oversight. But you didn't ask why."

"Because I Googled you that day," he mumbled, looking a little contrite. "Should I have waited?"

"No, you were the smarter one. Plus, you know, you have the whole family business you need to protect. But I'm not going to be a danger to any of that."

Though I did work for a man who hated him. However, that wasn't going to be a problem. This was just coffee, and Mr. Howard didn't care. They ran in different circles after all.

"I feel like I really should have asked your name."

"Maybe, but it was fun figuring out who you were just through text messages. I mean, I know that you don't like the Penguins."

I rolled my eyes. "I don't not like them. But you have to have loyalty. You're from here."

"I am. But sometimes I travel. And I can't get to an Avs game. Or a Broncos game."

"That is true. And honestly, I have no idea how you even got time away to have lunch today. You have to be too busy to have coffee today. What I know of your business is insane. You guys do so much."

He shrugged, tapping his finger on his mug. "True, and I have a good team and family that works with me. However, I'm allowed to have coffee with a beautiful woman."

I rolled my eyes. "That's a lie."

"It is not. I'm sorry to say, but you are beautiful."

"Well, I could say the same to you, but I'm pretty sure the two women that literally swooned next to you while we were talking in there answered that for both of us."

He snorted and finished his coffee. "I can't say that happens often."

"No you just don't notice it."

"So you didn't notice the man looking at you?"

"I only noticed you." I put my hand over my mouth and groaned. "Pretend I didn't say that."

"If it helps, I hadn't even realized I was standing there gawking at you until that woman said something," he whispered.

"Oh."

Oh.

"I really have to go back to work," I said after a moment, and he nodded.

"Same. I have meetings. But I'd like to do this again?"

My cheeks warmed. "Coffee in the middle of a workday?"

"Or dinner."

"Dinner. Dinner could be good."

He stood up and took my hand. "I'll text you?" he asked, the light in his eyes dancing.

I wanted to know this man. This enigma. "Okay. Text me." Texting him felt familiar in such an unfamiliar situation.

He kissed my hand again, and I rolled my eyes. "I'm sorry, I've never met someone who actually did that."

"I don't think I've ever actually done that," he said, squeezing my hand. "It just felt apropos."

"I'm busy this weekend," I blurted. "But maybe next weekend?"

"Next weekend can work, and as it happens, I'm busy as well."

"Well, this was nice, I'll talk to you soon?" I asked, knowing I was babbling at this point.

"Yes, Blakely, I'll talk to you soon. It was lovely to meet you in person. Especially for a wrong number." And then he walked away, and I did my best not to watch him do so.

Oh, I was in so much trouble.

Chapter 3
Blakley

"I cannot believe I'm back here at your house helping you choose what to wear. I don't think we've ever done that and yet here I am. Again."

I rolled my eyes at Isabella before taking a long look in the mirror. I wore a coral pink dress that had pockets and flared a bit. I was comfortable and it was one of my favorites, but it went to my knees, and looked a little too casual.

Isabella studied me in the mirror and tilted her head. "This is more of a sundress, right?"

"Not quite a sundress, but maybe like a day dress in the spring?"

She smiled. "And on a quiet first date in high school."

"Okay, so this dress is a no."

I quickly stripped out of my dress, and without even offering, Isabella took it from me. She immediately hung it up, and I picked up the next one.

"Okay, this one should work." It was a light blue chiffon sort of dress that went to my ankles, with a high slit. It had this lacy overlay that looked a little bit like tulle but really wasn't. The one strap was thin around my neck, and the other one was thick and made a bow at the neck.

"Is that a bridesmaid's dress?" Isabella asked.

I flushed, realizing I looked like Cinderella on a bender in this outfit.

"Yes. They make you buy these things and then say you can wear them again. But when can I wear this again? Do you see how much tulle-like fabric this has?" I asked, fluffing at the bow.

"I bet you my sister could fix it."

"She could?" I asked, eager.

"Of course. She's had to sew her costumes all the time. However, your gala is tonight. I don't think she's going to be able to rescue this in a few hours. Maybe for another event. Lord knows you go to enough of them."

I sighed and then stripped off the dress, getting tangled in the extra bow, and was grateful when Isabella turned her face from me so I couldn't see her laugh. "This isn't funny. I'm panicking."

"Don't panic. You have plenty of time."

I raised a brow and then looked at the clock on my bedside table. "I have three hours. Three hours to shower, figure out what I'm supposed to do with my hair, do my makeup, and make sure that I have the right shoes and bag for this. I don't think three hours is enough."

"Yes, because you're such an old hag it's going to take you forever."

"Thank you for understanding my pleas."

"Blakely, my best friend. You're going to be fine. You have so many dresses in here. We'll find you something. And I brought you a few as well."

"And I'm grateful. But I don't think my boobs are going to fit in it."

"Are you calling me small-chested?" Isabella asked, in her most prim of ice queen voices.

To most people Isabella was standoffish, a little rude, and very much protective of her family. She was literally called the ice queen by people at her job, and straight to her face. They didn't even bother to whisper the nicknames behind her back.

However, my best friend reveled in it. Because it kept people at a safe distance, and they treated her with respect at work. Maybe a little fear, maybe a little reverence, but respect.

I didn't mind that about her and found it more real and endearing than anything.

"Okay, what about this one?" I asked, picking up an A-line sage green dress.

"No. The slit's too high and I think there's a stain on it."

"Damn it. I thought I went to the dry cleaners with this. Maybe I forgot?"

"Maybe. You are busier than me most days."

I crossed my eyes, a little annoyed. "I have to remind myself that I like my job. But some days it's so hard."

"You don't like your job, you like what you're doing, and you just don't like the place of business. Hence why you had to work late today even though your boss wasn't there, and everyone's expecting you to be there tonight. All dressed up and fancy-free."

"What does fancy-free mean?" I asked, staring at her in the mirror as I held up my stained sage dress.

"I'm not sure. Let me look it up."

"Oh good. We can get lost in this. We can forget that I have to meet with humans tonight."

"You're great meeting with humans. I mean, you're always so personable, and everyone likes seeing you. Don't stress. You've got this."

"I have to go and schmooze so that way the boss can get more clients."

"That's what these events are for. But you've got this. We'll find you something to wear. You're beautiful, you have things to work with, and like I said, you're not too much of an old hag."

"Seriously, the love that I feel from you? I don't think I can hold back my yearning."

"One day we'll finally take each other wildly in the barn and no one will know our secrets."

We met gazes, before each bursting out in laughter, and she handed me a soft pink dress.

"What's this one?" I asked.

"It's mine. And it might not fit you in the boobs, mostly because you have a lot more than me."

"You're no slack there," I teased.

"You can talk all about them in the barn later," she whispered, wiggling her eyebrows.

"It's beautiful," I whispered, holding up the soft pink dress that would flow down to my ankles, barely brushing the floor if I wore the right heels.

"I've never seen you in this."

"I bought it for an event I never went to. So it's just been sitting in my closet. I should have given it to one of my sisters, since I figured they would wear it more than me, but I just haven't. So I get to give it to you. My other sister."

"Calling me your sister after saying you'll take me in the barn adds a whole new level to our fan fiction."

She cringed and gestured for me to try it on. "Let's see how it is on you. Hag."

I flipped her off, even as I began to slide on the dress. It fit perfectly in the waist, a heart-shaped neckline that accentuated my breasts. It had tiny straps that held the dress up and for that I was grateful.

"Well, it seems the dress was meant for you," she whispered.

I met her gaze in the mirror and swallowed hard. "It's gorgeous. But I don't want to take away the first time you ever wear it."

"It didn't look as good on me. We have different coloring. Honestly now, it should just be yours. I might take the sage green dress though. And see if I can get out the stain."

"You don't have to do that."

"It's my nemesis. Now, go take off that dress, and take a shower."

"Aw, I thought you were asking me to take off the dress for other reasons."

"We do not have time to learn all about our hidden places, Blakely. We have to get you ready for a gala. So do you think Mr. Cage will be there?"

I tripped over my own two feet, and she raised a brow at me, and I shook my head. "I'm sure *a* Cage will be there. His family does own one of the largest corporations in the city."

"I don't know too much about them, to be honest."

"Well they run in my circles. Or at least, in my boss's circles. And he hates them."

"Really?"

"I don't know why. But he always gets annoyingly growly about them, and he wants to beat them."

"So I take it you're not going to do lunch with him when he asks officially? Or dinner?"

"My boss or Aston?"

Isabella snorted. "Yes, Aston."

"I don't know. He's only texted a hello, but we've been busy. Nothing more."

"Well that's not fun."

"We have lives." I tried not to let the disappointment pepper my tone. He had said that he was busy all weekend, and so was I. Hence this event. It wasn't like I wanted to continue to flirt over texts with him. I didn't even know if I was going to go out with him. Although it had already come up as something we were going to do. A week from now.

"Well, just have fun. And what will you do if he is there though?" she asked, her voice soft as I stripped and got into the shower. I let the hot water run over my body as I thought about what I would do, and I didn't have an answer. That should have worried me more than anything.

"I'll say hello and be cordial. But this is a work event."

"So socializing with the Cages isn't in your repertoire?"

I washed my hair quickly, looking for more answers. "He probably won't even be there."

"If he was, would he bring a date?"

I nearly slipped in the shower, and glared at her as I looked around my shower curtain. "Really?"

She winced. "Sorry. I'm in a weird mood."

"Are you okay?" I asked, worried.

She waved me off and smiled. "I'm just fine.

Promise. We were talking about you. If he's there, you should dance. You said there was a spark."

"And my boss would absolutely hate it."

"So a win-win," she teased.

I shook my head. "Not so much if I want to keep my job."

"He can't fire you for flirting with a Cage."

"I'm sure he'd find a way about competing interests, or just any other way. He's not a nice man." My contract was year by year and though I was one of his best employees, I also outshone some of his "Yes Men" on occasion. I stood up to him, but there were always company politics. Therefore we had a dance and charity gala this evening. None of the others on staff were required to go. But the boss wanted to show off his employee in a dress so he could show the world how modern he was. Oh, he'd never say that, and no one would never outright point it out— but we all knew it was the case.

"Then why do you work for him?"

That was the question. And I wish I had better answers. "Because it's the best job I can get. And I'm sure a Cage will be there, but it's not going to be him. It's going to be one of his countless brothers."

"Okay, let's hope it's that way so you don't have to make a choice. At least in front of everyone."

I rinsed the conditioner out of my hair. "Nothing's ever easy."

"No. But that's life. Unending pain and suffering until you die."

I toweled off my hair, pausing to stare at her. "Is everything okay, Isabelle?" I asked, worry etched in my tone. "We don't have to talk about me all the time."

"I'm perfectly fine. I'm just razzing you. Now, let's get your hair done. And you know we talk about my family more often than not."

"Are you sure you have time for this?"

"I have time to help my best friend look hot in a dress for whoever might show up."

"He's not going to be there," I warned.

"Fine, I have time to help my friend look hot in a dress for herself. How about that?"

"Yes. Let's go with that."

It took an hour, but drying my hair, straightening it so I could curl it, and then doing a full face of makeup took time. Thankfully I had my grandmother's jewelry that I could make work with the dress, and when I finished the final clasp on my bracelet, I sighed in the mirror.

"Well, I don't look too shabby."

"You look beautiful. And don't stain my dress."

"I thought that I was being gifted this and you were taking the sage one?"

She smiled far too sweetly. "No, I'm just fixing the stain, and we can share both dresses. How about that?"

"You are a riot."

"I try. Now go knock them dead."

"Or at least try to win over clients. All in the name of finance," I said, sighing when Isabella rolled her eyes at me.

I drove myself to the event, because I was planning on only having one glass of champagne if that. I didn't want to deal with a ride-share or wait on anyone else. Thankfully there was a valet at the hotel, so I didn't have to find a way to park in this dress.

Holding my small clutch, I made my way into the hotel ballroom, smiling at a few people as I made my way around the room.

I saw a few familiar faces, though it was mostly strangers. When I caught the eyes of my boss's wife, she smiled softly at me and waved. I did not know how that sweet woman was married to that monster of a man, but then again, maybe he was only an asshole at work, and saved all his goodness for home.

The boss in question gave me a once-over and a tight nod, and I figured I'd passed some test.

A waiter passed by with a glass of champagne, and I milled about, holding my drink, barely taking a sip, and speaking with potential clients. I had already done research on the people that I knew I should talk to at the gala, the ones who had RSVP'd. But I hadn't seen a Cage on the list. Mostly because they were always invited, and they didn't have to RSVP to things like this.

That wasn't ominous at all.

"Well, small world."

It indeed was a small world. My hand squeezed on the stem of my champagne flute, and I turned around slowly, to stare into the eyes of Aston Cage.

"Oh. You're here."

He tilted his head and gave me that smile. The one that made my thighs clench, and I had to count backward from ten so I could catch my breath. "Yes, I'm here. The foundation is one that's close to my mother's heart. So we take turns attending different events. And it's my turn. Fancy that."

"I didn't know you'd be here."

He raised a brow. "And I didn't know you'd be here."

"Is it okay?" I shook my head. "Of course it's okay. This is work."

"You work for Howard, don't you?" he asked, his voice low. People really weren't paying attention to us other than the fact that their gazes would catch on Aston's. Because that's what the Cages did. They pulled in attention even when they weren't trying.

"I do."

"Is that going to be a problem?" he asked.

"Is what going to be a problem?" I asked, purposely obtuse. It wasn't as if we were making promises to each other or doing anything. I was just standing and speaking to a man at a gala, with a respectable distance between us. That's all that needed to be said.

"Well then, I'm glad that I'm the one who came, and not James."

"Which one was James on the text?" I asked, teasing.

"Probably the one trying to order us all."

"Wouldn't that be you?" I asked.

"That's what James would say," he replied, laughter in his gaze. Then a small pause. "Dance with me, Blakely," he whispered.

I shook my head. "I really shouldn't."

"There's many people on the dance floor, you can say you are schmoozing me."

"I don't think my boss would like that."

"Well, you should dance with me anyway. Please? I don't want to wait for a dinner date."

I couldn't see my boss anywhere, but I knew that this would probably get out. Because everything with the Cages did.

I set down my champagne flute on the table next to me anyway and placed my now free hand in his open one.

"Okay."

"Good." He clasped his hand over mine, and I was lost.

Chapter 4
Aston

GETTING HARD IN THE MIDDLE OF A BALLROOM while standing near many of my trustees, backers, and business rivals probably wasn't the best idea. But as soon as I saw Blakely across the dance floor, everything in me shifted.

And it wasn't just her beauty—those sharp cheekbones, those light eyes that shone underneath the soft lighting of the room. She'd even put her hair up in a half-do thing, so it framed her face, but still looked elegant. I used to be better about knowing what those were called, or even what kind of dress she wore. It had been a long time since I had been with anyone for that matter.

But no, it wasn't any of what she looked like, it

was the aura that seemed to surround her and others could feel it too. She may not have even realized they did. They stopped what they were doing to glance over at her, as if they wanted to know her. She'd catch everyone's attention, whether it be to judge her or to admire her.

Or in my case, to barely hold back from falling down on my knees in front of her.

And now she was mine. If only for this dance.

"So, I didn't realize this is what you would be doing this weekend," she said softly as we glided across the dance floor. She had her hand on my arm, her other clasping my own, and I smiled down at her.

I hadn't done this much smiling since my brother's wedding when they had all danced and partied and looked as if they actually were going to have a great time.

It was a little odd to think I was doing so now.

"We try to represent the family."

"Are you the only one here?"

I shook my head before I looked over hers to see both of my brothers raising their brows. Flynn and James had curious expressions on their faces, nearly identical even though neither one of them were the twins.

It must be odd to see me dancing with someone since I usually did not dance at these things. I smiled, spoke to those I needed to, did a speech if required, and wrote a check. I never got out on the dance floor when I came alone.

And yet here I was, with Blakely, losing my mind.

"Two of my brothers are here, they're behind you, staring at me and wondering why I'm dancing."

"You don't dance? You seem to be good at it."

The heat of her seared me through her dress and my tuxedo, and I had to swallow hard not to do anything that would shame us both. "I don't dance. I can, but I don't."

"Then why with me?" she asked, her voice a little breathy.

"I think you know, Blakely."

"So how many brothers do you have here?" she asked, changing the subject. I didn't mind, both of us needed to take a step to breathe if the way that her pulse fluttered against her neck was any indication.

"James and Flynn are here because it was our turn. My parents are out of town, or my mother and father would be here. Mother enjoys attending these events."

I hoped the bite wasn't in my tone at that, considering she liked all of her sons at these things so she could show us off.

"So three of you. That's a good number then."

I shook my head as I twirled her during the next song, both of us not having realized the song had even changed. "It's not even a full fifty percent. There are a lot of us."

"I knew you had a few brothers, but I hadn't really paid attention too much beyond that."

"There's more than a few of us. Not all of us work with Cage Enterprises though. However we do all have a stake in the company because it's our family. If that makes sense."

"Not in the slightest," she said with a laugh, her eyes shining.

"Understandable. We are here as a family to show our support, to donate, and to do what our family requires."

"I would say that sounds annoying, but you get to eat some decent food, and probably make business deals along the way."

I raised a brow at her but nodded. "Yes. That is always a perk. What about you? You're here with Howard Enterprises?"

I could feel eyes on me, and I knew it wasn't just

those who were curious who I was dancing with. No, the proprietor of Howard Enterprises was probably not happy about the woman who worked for him dancing in my arms. But there was nothing I could do about that. Nothing I wanted to do about that.

"Yes. Dancing with you is probably a mistake."

"He doesn't hate me that much, does he?" I asked, honestly curious.

"No. I don't think so. I think he just wants to one-up you."

"So does you dancing with me have anything to do with that?" I asked, oddly curious.

Her eyes narrowed, and she stopped dancing. I cursed under my breath and was grateful we were at the edge of the dance floor.

"I'm sorry. I didn't mean that."

"No you did. He didn't *ask* me to dance with you. You're the one who asked me to dance. And I knew it was going to be a mistake. He wants to beat you in everything all the time. So me dancing with the enemy probably isn't a good idea."

"I'm the enemy, am I?" I asked, my voice low.

She swallowed hard and shook her head. "No. It's not so dramatic as that."

"Good."

I lifted her hand up to my lips and kissed it again, a bare brush of my mouth against her skin, and her intake of breath was all I needed to hear.

"You need to stop doing that."

"I don't know if I want to."

Nobody was paying attention to us now, as the emcee was making their rounds, so I tugged on her hand and pulled her around the corner.

"Aston," she said with a laugh, and I did what I had been wanting to do since I first saw her. I pressed my lips to hers.

She didn't pull away, didn't freeze. Instead wrapped her fingers under the lapels of my jacket and pulled me closer.

Groaning, I deepened the kiss, my tongue sliding along hers.

"We need to stop. Someone can come around the corner at any minute."

"I'll stop. Soon." I kissed her again, needing her taste, craving her, and when I knew that it would be too much if I continued, I wrenched myself away, my chest rising and falling in deep pants.

"Holy hell," I growled.

"Oh."

I looked over at Blakely, her hand over her

bruised lips, her eyes wide. "Are you okay? Did I hurt you?"

"Not at all. I don't think I've ever been kissed like that before. Which probably isn't something I should say." I had barely any control when it came to her.

I felt like a cat who caught the canary, and a smile slid across my face. "That sounds like a compliment."

"Maybe. Or maybe I need to get out more." She grinned up at me.

Her eyes danced, and I wanted to know more. I wanted to know everything.

Who was this woman? And why did she do this to me?

"Sorry to interrupt, but they need you." I cursed at Flynn's timing, and Blakely's face drained of color, while she tried to hide behind a potted palm.

"It's just my brother. Everything's fine."

"I'm so embarrassed. I'm *working* for God's sake."

"It's okay, nobody saw. James and I had the exits covered."

"Should it worry me that it sounds like you guys have a plan for this sort of thing?" she asked, slight frost in her tone.

CARRIE ANN RYAN

I cursed my brothers and everything they stood for, while I glared at him and James who walked up from behind him. "No, this is new. But we protect our family."

Flynn looked over my shoulder and winked at Blakely. "I'm Flynn. The quiet one here is James. It's good to see you."

"Hi. I'm going to go fix my face. And then I have to…work."

"You look wonderful," James said softly, and I glared at him before turning my back to them and looking at Blakely.

"I have to go be The Cage," I said with a roll of my eyes.

"I love the title." I heard the humor in her tone —even above the slight panic.

"I don't," I said softly. "I want to see you again."

Her eyes widened marginally. "Okay. Maybe not in the middle of a hallway?"

"No. Let's not. I'll call you."

When she let out a soft laugh, I relaxed. Marginally. "Good. And then I'll have my wits about me."

"I need to go." Long before this.

"He really does," Flynn called out.

"Then go," she whispered.

And then I pressed my lips to hers again before

letting her walk away, presumably to go fix the blush of her face. But I thought she looked gorgeous.

"So, have you lost your mind?" Flynn asked as we stepped out of earshot.

"Stop it. I don't want to hear it."

Flynn clucked his tongue. "I think you've lost your mind."

"I think you're more like Dorian than we thought," James whispered, and I flipped them both off, before straightening my jacket.

"Let's go be Cages and do what we need to."

"So that's the girl from the chat?" James asked.

I nodded tightly. "We're done here."

"Oh, I think you've just begun," Flynn said with a laugh.

I rolled my eyes at my two brothers, and moved toward the ballroom, knowing we had people to meet, and there was work to be done. My phone buzzed in my pocket however, and I couldn't help but hope it was her.

However it wasn't Blakely calling, it was my mother.

"Answer it, or we're all going to have to deal with that," Flynn said with a roll of his eyes.

I sighed but answered anyway. "Hello, Mother. You're missing a great gala."

"Aston. It's your father."

Ice slid up my spine, and I swallowed hard. I must have looked as if something was wrong, because both my brothers stopped teasing me, and stood still, staring at me.

"What's wrong?"

"Your father is dead. And I need you here. Call the others. We need you." She hung up without saying anything else, and I stared at my brothers knowing everything had changed.

Chapter 5

Blakely

He hadn't called.

He should have called. But he hadn't.

I waited by my phone for four days, waiting for a call. The weekend had passed, and then the holiday where there was no work, just me waiting by a phone as I sat at home alone.

But he hadn't called.

I had picked up my phone countless times to call him, but he had said he would call me. And he was Aston Cage, man of business. I wasn't going to be the one who called first. Right?

Phone in hand, I knew I just needed to put on my big-girl panties and do it. I looked up his texts, pressed his icon, and called.

It rang once and went straight to voicemail. I frowned but didn't leave a message.

He had sent me straight to voicemail. Maybe he was in a meeting? Or maybe he just wasn't calling.

I knew I needed to get to work, and I had to stop stressing over the fact that a man hadn't called me after he had kissed the daylights out of me in the middle of a work function.

That was so unprofessional it wasn't even funny. I had gone right back to work, spoken to the clients I needed to, and made a few business deals for my boss. I had done what I was supposed to do, and yet everything felt different.

I felt different.

I sighed and went to finish my breakfast as I turned on the morning news. I needed to leave soon so I wouldn't be late, but everything felt off.

This just in, Dorian Cage the patriarch of the Cage family is dead at age sixty. He was the former president of Cage Enterprises and Businesses, a worldwide and billion-dollar firm of real estate development, small business backers, environmental research, including dozens of other subsidiaries. And while he wasn't at the helm of the business at the time of his death, with his eldest son Aston Cage taking that position, he was still the man on the mountain for many. However it seems that his death, while of natural causes, did not come without a scandal of its own.

There's more to come on this once we have all of the information, but according to inside sources, the Cage family has its secrets.

Everything froze within me as I stared at the TV and tried to understand what I was hearing.

Aston's father was dead.

No wonder he couldn't call or text. His father was dead.

And a scandal? I didn't even want to know exactly what that was, but I couldn't even imagine.

I picked up my phone again and knew that he was far too busy for me, but I needed to text. Needed to say something. Anything.

ME:

> I'm so sorry, Aston. I can't imagine your loss. My thoughts are with you and your family. And if there's anything you need from me, ever, let me know. I'm sorry.

I sent the text, hoping it was enough, even though it would never be. Maybe he would see it and remember. But I was just the girl from the texts, a woman that he saw on the dance floor and kissed.

No wonder he hadn't called.

Tears pricked my eyes, as emotions washed over me, but I knew that it was silly.

This wasn't about me. He had the most obvious reason not to call.

I gathered my things and headed to work, and knew that I was going to have to find a way to either get over Aston Cage, or make sure he wasn't alone. Because from what I could tell, as the eldest, he had the weight of the world on his shoulders.

Or maybe I was thinking too hard, and I had nothing to do with it. It was all just a dream. Before I knew who he was.

I walked into work, and I realized that people were staring at me. It was odd, to feel the weight of a thousand stares, but I ignored them, and made my way to my desk.

"Blakely, come inside my office," Mr. Howard ordered, his voice deep, commanding. Ice slid down my back, but I swallowed hard, sitting my bag on the table, and wondering why he was here so early, and why he could want me first thing.

I lifted my chin, and ignored the stares of others, as I made my way to his office.

"Hello, Mr. Howard, good morning. What can I do for you?"

"You're fired."

I blinked at him, caught off guard. "What?"

"You're fired for working with the competition. We lost the Meridian account to the Cages, and that happened right after your little dance with him. We can connect the dots and have done so."

I schooled my features, hoping my racing heart didn't beat out of my chest. "What? I have nothing to do with that."

"Oh? So it's just a coincidence that we lost the biggest account that we have to the Cages right after you went on a little dance break and whatever else with the head of the company? What else did you say when you were sleeping with him?" he spat before his lawyer shut him up.

Rage filled me, as bile crept up my throat. "I didn't do anything…"

"We have evidence to say different," one of the lawyers said, and I glared at him, and realized that they were going to find any reason to get me out. They were going to lie and twist the narrative, and I wouldn't be able to fight back. I could sue. I could plead my case. And yet no one would listen to me.

Because I had danced with Aston Cage, and I had apparently made a fool of my boss.

"I didn't do this," I repeated.

"And I don't believe you," Mr. Howard said before gesturing to his lawyers and security to escort me out.

People continued to stare, as I realized this was my reality.

I had made one mistake—dancing with a gorgeous man who made me smile.

And even though I could find my own lawyers, and I could find a way to get out of a wrongful termination suit, they would find another way to push me out.

Out of a job I hated—out of a job that broke me.

And somehow this was Aston Cage's fault.

Because this was before I knew. Before I knew him. Before I knew how much I could feel.

And before I knew how much I could break.

Aston Cage was out of my life. Only the scars of that one dance with a Cage would shroud my life and my future.

I hoped he never called.

I had made enough mistakes when it came to Aston Cage.

And I would never make them again.

Start the Cage Family series and find out what
happens with Aston and Blakely in:
The Forever Rule

A Note from Carrie Ann Ryan

Thank you so much for reading **Before I Knew.**

The text message idea came to me while doing laps in the pool and wondering why my phone kept going off on the table. It turns out 11(!) of my group chats were all having conversations and I had to catch up. Then I wondered what would happen if I didn't know these lovely people and I jumped into a conversation mid-rant haha.

The Cage Family series is already one of my favorites I've ever written for the sheer fact that it's one of the hardest!

I know you want Blakely and Aston's story and you can read their HEA in The Forever Rule!!

The Cage Family

Book 1: The Forever Rule

Book 2: An Unexpected Everything

Book 3: If You Were Mine

Start the Cage Family series in full with:
The Forever Rule

If you want to make sure you know what's coming next from me, you can sign up for my newsletter at www.CarrieAnnRyan.com; follow me on twitter at @CarrieAnnRyan, or like my Facebook page. I also have a Facebook Fan Club where we have trivia, chats, and other goodies. You guys are the reason I get to do what I do and I thank you.

Make sure you're signed up for my MAILING LIST so you can know when the next releases are available as well as find giveaways and FREE READS.

Happy Reading!

A NIGHT
for US

CARRIE ANN
RYAN

NEW YORK TIMES BESTSELLING AUTHOR

A Night for Us

Eli Wilder is at a loss. Due to tragedy, time, and life in general, he and his five brothers are suddenly getting out of the military at the same time.

Only none of them have any idea what to do next.

Eli might have a plan—one so far-fetched it will take a miracle for them to agree to it.

When he takes a chance, however, he meets the perfect woman. One he hadn't expected.

Now he has one night to prove he's the right man for the job—and for her.

Chapter 1
Eli

HOME IS WHERE THE HEART IS. OR MAYBE JUST where you rest your boots after a long day. A long week. Hell, a long twenty years.

I wasn't even forty years old yet, and here I was, retired. Or at least as retired as one could be after putting in twenty with the military. I had put my entire life and career towards one goal, and now I was out. There was no going back. I was never going to work for the military again as a civilian or get a GS—general scale—position. I was just me… in this house I was renting because I wasn't sure where I wanted to live, but it was my home for now.

My boots were in the closet, scuffed and worn, and most likely headed towards the trash pile.

But I wore my new boots, ones that I was just now wearing in, getting to fit around my feet. And I had a roof over my head, and I suppose my heart was in it. Therefore, this was home.

I pinched the bridge of my nose and let out a breath. I clearly needed more coffee if I was going to pick apart a saying and add poetry of my own.

"Why did you ask us over here if you're just going to growl at yourself the whole time?" Evan asked from the doorway into the kitchen, and I turned to see my brother standing there, his posture rigid, slight lines of pain around his eyes. He was still getting used to the new prosthetic, but with therapy and a whole shit-ton of doctors, Evan was able to stand here in my kitchen on his own accord, with a glare on his face. Of course, the glare had always been there, even before the IED.

"Seriously though, are you going to come in with the rest of us? We got the barbecue."

"From Harmon's?" I asked, my stomach rumbling.

"Of course we got it from Harmon's," Everett called out from the living room, and I snorted before grabbing the six-pack of beer I had for this occasion.

I followed Evan out of the kitchen and into the

living room, where Everett, Elijah, East, and Elliot were already lounging. We could have sat in a dining room, but I didn't have a large enough table for us. So we would be sprawling on my worn couch and used armchairs. I hadn't been able to get furniture of my own all my life. Or at least my adult life. I had moved from place to place, starting out in the barracks, and then I used rented furniture from the military because I was either overseas or living on base. When I had moved off base, I had put most of my money away and hadn't bothered with expensive furniture. Now I had furniture that I got from thrift stores and garage sales. Most guys I knew my age and rank had household items that didn't look like they belonged to a young bachelor. But all of them were married and had families. I'd run from mine.

"What is with this couch?" Elijah asked, sitting nearly ramrod straight at the edge of it. "We're adults now. Shouldn't you have something that isn't so brown and lumpy that you can sink into?"

Evan grunted as he sat into the armchair, resting his leg straight out in front of him. "This chair isn't that bad, but it's not good."

I flipped them both off as I handed everybody a beer and took a seat on the floor. I may be the eldest here, but my brothers had already claimed the chairs, so I was stuck with this. "Honestly, I was just thinking that I needed new shit, but first, I need a house. One that's not a rental."

"It's still a good time for the market," Elliot put in, looking down at his phone. He bounced his foot quickly as he spoke, and I held back a snort at that.

"I know it's a good time in the market." That was a decent segue, so I let out a breath. "However, I don't want to buy a house."

East's eyes widened. "What do you want to buy?"

I looked at my brothers, at the five of them that were my best friends. Between them and our youngest sister Eliza, there were seven of us. All named with an E, and all different in the same way. Somehow all six of us brothers had joined the Air Force and had rarely lived in the same place. It was hard enough to find a position that worked for you in the military for long, let alone finding a place that was near one of your siblings. It just didn't work out that way. I had been on tour at the same time with at least one sibling, but we were never stationed in the same place. They did that on purpose, from back in the days when wars would take out entire squadrons, and therefore an entire set of siblings. But I still felt like it had been years since I'd really gotten to know my brothers. Now we were all in the same place, *retired*.

Evan didn't want to be here, but I knew it wasn't because of family. No, he had his own reasons for not wanting to move back to San Antonio. We had lived here before when we had been kids, the seven of us, and it felt like home when we'd been little. We could have moved out west to where our uncles had lived on the winery, but that hadn't felt right. Now we were here in Texas trying to make our own home.

San Antonio had enough bases, so many military people retired in the area. It was gorgeous, decent weather if you liked the heat, and it was within driving distance of hill country, wine country, desert, city, and even the beach if you wanted to drive around five hours. It was a good area, and I was glad that this was where we were putting down our roots.

Although, Eliza wasn't moving down with us. When the guys and I had all planned where we were going to retire, I had always assumed Eliza would come with us. And then she had lost her husband in an IED explosion, the catalyst for why all of us Wilders had gotten out when we had.

Between Evan's accident, and Eliza's husband's,

we hadn't wanted to stay in anymore. I had reached my twenty while the others hadn't, but we were all out. Though Eliza had found love again somehow and was up in Fort Collins with her husband's family. I didn't begrudge her for that, and I knew we would all be visiting our little sister often, but it was still odd that she wasn't going to be with us.

Either way, though, we were here—the Wilder brothers. Evan was growly and not exactly pleasant at the moment. It had nothing to do with his pain, though, and all to do with his past.

Everett liked it here, at least from what I could tell. He was the quietest of us all, and sometimes it was hard for me to figure out exactly what he was thinking at all times.

Elijah was out of his depth and angry but always had a smile on his face. He was also the only one that actually liked wearing a suit, so maybe he would like what I had in store for us. I wasn't sure, though.

East knew what he wanted, though he never told us. He was growly, a little abrasive, but considering what he used to do, it worked for him. But I knew he needed roots, needed to settle with us, and so that's why we were here. To keep him safe. To keep all of us safe. Including Elliot, the youngest of the brothers, though still older than Eliza by a couple of years. He had gone out earlier than all of us for his own reasons. And I knew of all of them. He was going to click with what I had in mind more than the rest. At least, that's what I hoped.

"Seriously? Why are we here?" Evan growled and then let out a sigh.

I figured I might as well tell them what my plans were, even if they felt insane. "I don't plan on living in this house for long. It's a rental, and I do want to buy. Just not a house."

"You said that, but what do you mean?" Everett asked as he leaned forward over our meal.

"I want to buy land."

They blinked up at me, and Evan tilted his head. "You want to be a rancher? Or just buy land with a lot of oaks?"

I snorted, thinking of the land for sale around us. The market was hot and many people moving out here wanted the land for privacy, not necessarily for what it had been used for in the past. "The place I'm looking at has a few oaks, but not a ranch. No, I want to buy land that is far more expensive than what I can afford alone."

They all looked at me then, while Elijah leaned forward. His normal smile tilted down, and he frowned. "You mean the inheritance? From our uncles?"

Our mother's brothers had both passed within the last year, and we were the only family that they had. When they died, their winery had been sold, as required by the will, but the proceeds from it, as well as whatever holdings they had, went to *us*. Meaning we had a decent nest egg on its way, and none of us had been expecting it or planning on it. So I had plans of my own. I just had to hope that they agreed.

"There's a piece of land that I want to buy. And I want to make it a retreat. Or, rather, continue the property as a retreat with our own touches."

"What the hell are you talking about?" Evan snarled.

"Yeah, you want to spend money that we don't have yet? I mean, I know it was out of the blue, but what the fuck?" East put in.

I held up my hand. "We all need something to do. Right now, we're working in dead-end jobs to give us an income and to pay our bills, but none of us were expecting to get out when we did." I looked at all of them, and they swallowed hard, nodding.

"It's hard to find a new career when you thought you already had one," Elijah whispered.

Elijah had been a meteorologist for the Air Force, but the degree he had finally been able to get wasn't in meteorology. It was hard to find a job in the field that he was trained in when he didn't have the right degree for a civilian. But he was brilliant in more than that, and I hoped he realized that.

"Just let me finish," I began. "I want to open up a retreat. A Wilder Retreat. And the land that I'm looking at, the land I've already spoken to the owners about, is a place where we can make it an inn. Host weddings, and there's even a winery attached. The owners are fine with wanting to change the name of the company, too. I wouldn't have done it if they'd had a strong connection to it. We can make Wilder fucking Wines." They all looked at me like I was insane, and maybe I was. But I had plans. "Before you think I've lost my mind, I've been talking to Roy."

"Roy, wait, didn't he open up a place like it outside of Austin?" Everett asked, frowning.

"He did. That's where I got the idea. We all need something to do, and we've all been living on our own and away from each other for long enough that it feels like we're not even the same brothers anymore." They were all silent so I kept going. "I want us to work together. I want us to start a business."

"The Wilder Retreat," Evan growled. "What's our tagline? Let loose and get wild?"

I ran my hand through my hair, knowing our dinner was getting cold, but I had started about this the wrong way. "Fuck I don't know. But we plan things. We can do this."

Everett moved forward. "We're military. We trained in explosives and planes. We don't do wineries or fucking weddings or winery tours."

They were all saying things I had gone over in my head countless times, but the thing was, we were more than our past, and I had to hope to hell we figured that out. "I know that. But we can learn. The place that I'm looking at, the owner is an older man who wants to sell, and there's already staff in place that know what they're doing. We can fit in, find our way. We are more than just the jobs that we were given and trained for all our lives. We can do this. And we need a normal."

"And this would be a normal?" Elliot asked, but I saw the interest in his eyes.

"What do you want us to do for the rest of our lives? Work a desk job? Work for someone else? We've been working for someone else our entire lives. Let's work for ourselves. Let's make it our business."

"What would we do?" Evan asked, his voice low.

"We'll split the business. Each of us would have our own concept of what we're doing. We've all been in charge of organizing and setting up plans and strategizing. Our jobs as teens were like this, even if it's been a few years for some of us. Now, instead of the way that we operated in the military, we'll put it to use for running an inn and a winery."

"I like the taste of wine. I don't actually know how to make wine," Evan whispered.

I shook my head. "Of all of us, you know the most about wine. You worked with the uncles over our summers as a teen and even again every time you visited on whatever vacations you could take over the years."

Evan scowled. "Yeah, so I know a little bit, but I don't know enough to begin a new wine. I only know about the grapes from their place, not these."

"We are near Fredericksburg. They make great wines," Everett said, his eyes narrowing. Everett was brilliant. If he hadn't gone into the service, I knew he would have been an accountant or his own

CEO or CFO. I knew he'd be the one to make sure that we didn't go bankrupt. He just didn't know it.

"Evan, they have a vintner, a winemaker. But they need someone to help as the Director. What Uncle Leo used to do and what you trained for before you joined up." Evan scowled at me, but it didn't look as menacing at least.

"So, what, we each get our own position and we figure out how to work together?" East asked, growling. "I'm good with my hands. I can build things. I don't want to work in hospitality or with fucking grapes."

I nodded tightly. "I know that East. So that could be your job. Things break down, and we need to build things. I have all this written out, and I was going to talk it over with you. But first, I want to make sure that's something that's feasible. On top of that, Roy invited us to a wedding."

"We're not fucking wedding planners," Evan growled.

I held up my hand. "That's why we would hire a wedding planner for that part. As for an event planner? I think we all know who among us could be that person. We could be the people that show off our area. To plan tours for the winery, or even downtown San Antonio, or anything for when somebody wants to relax. We have spent our whole lives working for the government, risking our lives. Now, let's enjoy it. Enjoy a home that we can build. And help others relax, too. I know it's insane. But I didn't want us to work together in a bar or build a company from the ground up. This place is already settled, and it has potential. We can hire someone for the wedding part, someone good. But we can do the rest."

"And Roy wants you to visit him then?" Elijah asked, speaking of my friend who had gotten out a couple of years before me, and had sparked this idea.

"He has a very similar concept a couple of hours from us. I want to see how it works, and you should come with us."

"So, we're going to crash a wedding?" Everett asked.

"Well, I was thinking you and I could. And at least take some notes. Everyone else has to work, and I figured some of you guys might not be in the mood for a wedding."

Evan grunted, and we all knew who I was talking about at that moment.

"This is insane," Elijah began, but held up his hand when I started to interrupt. "But I could see it.

We've all talked about getting out and working together. We just happened to get out far sooner than we planned."

There was silence in that, but we were good about not talking about the whys of it.

"So we're going to start over, work for ourselves, and we have the money to do this?" Everett asked as he pulled out his phone and started running numbers.

"We do. I hope. I'll send you what I have. The owner doesn't have any kids and wants to sell. He also wants to keep the business that he already has in place operating. He's one of us. Retired Air Force."

That made Evan's lips twitch. "I guess we can listen to him then."

I knew that would get Evan. We were a brother-hood, even those not by blood. I didn't know if this was going to work or if it was just a lark.

I wanted us to be together. I wanted us to work towards a common purpose. And if that meant going out on a limb and trying something completely crazy and something that could risk everything, then I would do it. We had risked our lives for longer than I cared to admit. Why not risk something else to find a home?

In order to be settled.

Everett and I could see Roy and realize that this wasn't what we wanted, and we'd find something else. This had shown up out of the blue, and it just spoke to me.

I was probably losing my goddam mind, but I didn't have anything else.

I wanted my brothers settled, and I was the eldest. I needed to make sure that they were safe and had a future. None of us were married, other than Eliza. None of us had a family. We had spent so long protecting others. Now it was time to think for ourselves.

So we would. And I would make sure that they had a path—that they had a future.

First, however, it was time to go to a wedding.

Chapter 2
Alexis

MY JOB WAS TO PLAN. AND YET, I DIDN'T THINK I could prepare for this.

"I just really wanted the sun to shine from the goddess on my wedding. And yet it feels as if she's crying." The bride paced in front of me, her hair in hot rollers, her eyes puffy from sobbing. I risked a look behind her at the bright sun and the single white puffy cloud in the sky. The cloud that was apparently sending this woman over the edge.

"It will be okay. The weather is still on our side." I knocked on wood as I said it, knowing that's what she wanted me to do. And frankly, I would have done it anyway.

"Do you see that cloud? That cloud is mocking me on this day. It is mocking everything that I have stood for. Now how will I know if my love is true, knowing this cloud exists? I was supposed to be wed. To blend my soul with that of my mate and to know that our forever was only a beginning. And yet, it is over. Everything is over." She flung herself on the chaise lounge while her mother glared at me before patting her daughter's arm.

"We'll find a way to make this work. I know it's going to be hard, but don't you worry. We will find a way."

The bride began to sob in earnest. "Today was supposed to be about love and prosperity. I saw it happen."

I nodded even though she couldn't see me and knelt by her, putting on my best wedding planner tone. "Of course, it's about love and prosperity. You are going to marry the love of your life this afternoon."

"Will I? Or will that cloud ruin my destiny? For I was told that today was the day that we were supposed to be married. I saw it in the cards, as did my psychic. Don't you see? She told me today was the day."

I sat back on my heels and nodded sagely at her words, trying not to roll my eyes. I was of the mind that people were allowed to believe in whatever they wanted to, that there was more than one possibility for the world we were in.

And yet, right then, it was all a little too much for me. Mostly because everything had been planned by me, and therefore the psychic. The psychic had chosen this day for the wedding, so I had agreed to it. The psychic had read what color the wedding needed to be in tea leaves, so I had gone with it. My job was to make sure the bride was happy, and the groom as well, but mostly the bride in this case.

The groom just seemed happy that his bride had said yes after years of trying to get her to commit, and therefore I was here. To work on the Baylor Ranch and Brewery and to plan this wedding.

I truly loved this venue. Roy Baylor, the owner and operator of the retreat and venue was a wonderful man, a little strict, but knew what he wanted. And that meant making sure that the bride was happy.

Even if a single cloud in the sky was about to ruin her day, apparently.

"Okay now, let's think about what this cloud can signify," I began as my assistant walked in, her eyes wide at the scene in front of her. I waved her off, and Emily slowly backed out of the room, trying not to make a noise so she wouldn't get caught.

At least she was allowed to leave. Maybe she would be able to work with the caterer, the venue, and to ensure everything else was on track for the wedding that was supposed to begin in forty-five minutes.

I smiled softly and did what I did best: made the bride happy. "That single cloud can be evidence of the path you were once on. The path of you as a woman. But it is showing you that you are ready for the next phase. To the blue skies that will be your marriage." Emily gave me a thumbs-up as she walked out, and I did think that I had done pretty well just then in terms of making crap up.

"Do you think? Do you think that Reggie will be okay with this? That he won't leave me because of this cloud and what it can signify?"

. I leaned down in front of Phoenix and held her hand. "You are a beautiful bride. Exquisite. You are marrying the love of your life. I cannot wait to see you in that dress and to watch the reaction of the love of your life as he sees you for the first time today."

She patted her lip, her pout slowly decreasing. "It is a beautiful dress."

"And you are the beautiful woman in that dress. He is going to marry you, not because of the signs, but because he loves you. And that cloud is not the shadow upon your day. It is just a mere moment in time, signifying it is the next phase of your life. It is time for you to marry your Reggie. For Reggie and Phoenix to have a wedding on the books like no other."

I wasn't lying then. This would be a wedding like no other.

"Do you think?" she asked as her mother continued to wipe tears from her face.

"I do. Now let's get you finished with your hair and makeup. And then in that dress. Reggie's waiting. Much like that cloud was waiting for you to see it so it could depart, and you can know that your day is in perfect harmony."

One of the bridesmaids rolled her eyes, and I gently narrowed mine, warning her not to say anything. She grinned wide, and I ignored her and went to help the bride finish getting ready. Knowing she was in good hands with the rest of the wedding party, I went to my other duties, focusing on the caterer and whatever else came up.

The best man walked past, his face a little too bright, and I leaned forward and handed him a mint and a bottle of water from the side table. "Eat this and drink this. No more pregaming before the wedding."

He smiled at me, a little sloppily. "Yeah, I know. I'm just trying to walk it off."

That was good to hear, at least. "No worries, we will make sure that this wedding is amazing. Just stay a little more hydrated."

"You've got it, boss. Thanks, Ms. Alexis."

I waved him off. "It's what I'm here for."

The venue had its own florist and caterer, so I didn't have to use my contacts, which was nice. Not all venues had that, nor did they have their own planning stations. I liked working with places like that felt as if they were resorts. Those didn't tend to have an on-hand wedding planner, but an event planner where I could step in and do my part of the job. Sometimes it got a little hard to mix the two, but Jeff and I worked well together. Right now, he was working on another event for the company while I was working on this wedding. Some guests at the resort weren't part of the wedding itself, and so it was Jeff's job to make sure that they had something to do that would not interfere with the wedding. Now mine was all about the ceremony and following reception. I checked over the cake one more time and made sure everybody was in their place.

"Blue alert, blue alert," Emily said into my headset, and I held back a sigh.

"Blue?" I asked as I made my way to her.

"It's not quite urgent, but it does have to do with the color of the bridesmaids' dresses," Emily whispered fiercely as I came to her side.

"What is it?" I asked, and then I didn't need her to explain.

One of the bridesmaids, Jasmine, if I remembered correctly, was not wearing the correct dress. Oh, it was the right color, but it used to have far more fabric than it currently did.

"Crap on a cracker," I mumbled.

Emily blinked. "Is that the saying?"

"It is now. Okay, let me handle this." I rolled my shoulders back and smiled as Emily went to deal with another part of our checklist. I looked at Jasmine as the other woman just narrowed her gaze, put her hand on her hip, and showed off a generous amount of leg.

"You can't tell me what to do," Jasmine snapped, and from there, I knew that the other woman had planned this on purpose because she wanted to be the showcase of the day.

Well, screw that. This was what I was good at and what I was going to fix.

"You look wonderful, Jasmine. Though the dress is a little bit different than what we had planned on, correct?"

"Oh, I had always planned on this. Phoenix has always been a little too much. You know? This will put her down a peg."

I smiled through my teeth, even as my eyes went cold. Jasmine must have seen the look because her hand fell, and she raised her chin defiantly. "Today is about Phoenix. And Reggie. And their love for one another. While you do look amazing, this is not the dress you agreed on."

"There's no way you can add more to it. I've already had it altered."

I nodded tightly. "Oh, I know. However, when there's a will, there's a way."

I looked to the side as Emily came running

forward, our seamstress right beside her. "Now come on, I know exactly what you need to do."

"There's not enough time," Jasmine snapped.

"Arabella is brilliant at what she does. We'll make the time."

Arabella's eyebrows winged to the top of her forehead as she took in the gown. "It's a good thing I've brought extra fabric. You never know when you're going to need to add an entire skirt."

The defiance on Jasmine's gaze didn't alter. "You will not be touching me or my dress."

I raised a brow. "And if you continue to think that way, you will not be in the wedding."

"This is not your day. You don't get to tell me what to do." Her lower lip wobbled and while I wondered what might have happened between the two women in the past to lead them here, my job was to ensure the bride was happy without hurting anyone in the process. Finding that balance was a tap dance.

Thankfully I'd taken lessons.

"No, this is Phoenix's day. And actually, I do get to tell you what to do. This is not the same dress that the others had decided on, therefore, you will have to wear something appropriate for Phoenix. I'm not going to tell you what's appropriate in general or in life, just what the bride wants. And today is about what the bride wants."

"She's just going to get divorced in a minute anyway. She and Reggie aren't even good for each other. He liked me first."

This wasn't something I was going to get into. I didn't have it in me. Nor did I care. I turned toward the seamstress and gave her a genuine smile. "Thank you, Arabella."

Arabella grinned. "Don't you worry. I'll get it taken care of."

"You're not listening to me," Jasmine snapped, and I tilted my head and smiled at her, knowing it didn't quite reach my eyes.

"Today is not about you. Or me. This is about the bride and the groom. This is their moment. You don't get to ruin it. Even if you might feel differently. When it is over, you can have a lovely talk with Phoenix, and I will understand. But for now, you will fix your dress, you will walk down the aisle and smile, and you will be the beautiful woman that I know you are, inside and out." That was stretching it a bit, but with the way that Jasmine's eyes warmed slightly, I had to hope that that was the right trick. "You can do this, Jasmine. You can show the world that you can handle anything."

"He was mine," Jasmine murmured.

My heart hurt for her, even though I was slightly cold inside when it came to love these days. Not that I was going to mention that. "But he's hers now. And you said yes to the wedding. Be a good friend. Show that you love them both."

"Fine," Jasmine snapped and turned to follow Arabella.

"That was one disaster levied," Emily whispered just by my side, and I nodded tightly.

"We'll keep an eye on her."

"I'll do that since you have the other thousand things to do."

I shook my head. "We'll do it together. We have twenty minutes until go time. Time to go through our checklist one more time."

We nodded at each other then went to work, fixing the maid of honor's shoe and then the flower crown for the flower girl. The ring bearer currently had his finger halfway up his nose, so I helped wash his hands and anchored him to one of the groomsmen who could handle the kid. I walked from pew to pew, ensuring that each flower arrangement was where it needed to be, and as the minister nodded at me, a gentle smile on his face, I knew we were almost there.

So close.

Roy stopped me on my way to the bride and grinned. "Good job, Alexis."

I smiled at the older man and shook my head. "Not yet. Almost there, though."

"Of course, can't put the cart before the horse and all that."

"You sound more and more Texan every day." I winked.

He let out a rough chuckle. "I try. Now, I'll see you after the wedding. Save me a dance."

I rolled my eyes, knowing Roy was happily married but was doing his best to try to get me out on the dance floor because apparently I needed to have a life. I had a life, thank you very much. It just didn't have anything to do with weddings. Other than the fact that my entire life was weddings. Just not my own.

Once the wedding began, I had my eyes on every person that I could at the same time, narrowing them at Jasmine as she walked in her now full gown, Arabella's magic to die for. Jasmine looked like a princess herself, a little manic, but didn't ruin the wedding. And when Phoenix walked down the aisle underneath the blue skies—without a single cloud—I smiled and let out a relieved breath.

The first part was now over, now for the actual reception where things were just getting started.

My photographer was set up for photos, and I let Emily handle half of them when I ensured that the rest of the wedding guests were doing their thing in the reception. They were going for a buffet, so people could mingle and party about, and the dance floor would be rocking soon. First, though, we had a few other things to handle, and I was exhausted. I should probably sleep a little bit more before big weddings, but I had too much on my plate.

When the bride and the groom made their entrance, I smiled, and Emily wiped away a tear.

"They're just so beautiful."

"They are," I agreed. I also didn't think they would last long, but maybe they would surprise me. I liked when they surprised me. I wanted love to last, even though sometimes it didn't, and it broke you.

Emily nudged me, and I looked over at her, shaking my head. "What? Is something wrong?"

"Look over at *them*. All tall, dark, and handsome. And growly. I want to take a bite of that. Who are they?"

I laughed. I couldn't help it. One of the guests

gave me a look and smiled, and I held back a wince. My job was to blend into the scenes, not to make noise and laugh. I had to be better than that.

I stared over at the two men with dark hair and blue eyes and frowned. I didn't recognize them, and I had to wonder what side of the wedding they were from. I frowned, going through my mental list, but figured they had to be someone on the groom's side since I didn't know everybody by their face. However, they seemed to be brothers and were attractive, though I didn't swoon like Emily seemed to be doing. Barely.

"Seriously though, who are they? And are they single?"

"You can find out after the wedding. We do not mix pleasure with business. You know that."

Emily put her hand over her heart and mimicked it beating while she fluttered her eyelashes at me. "Don't you wish we did, though?" she purred, and I shook my head before I met the gaze of the slightly older man. His blue eyes intensified and narrowed on mine before a shiver went down my spine. I swallowed hard, and broke the connection, and looked down at Emily.

"Not for us. You know that."

"Spoilsport. But I suppose we have to get back to work."

I swallowed hard and then looked back to where the man had been standing, only to find the space empty, and sighed. "Time to work. It's what we're good at."

And I pushed the thoughts of the man with the blue eyes from my mind, knowing I had far more important things to worry about tonight.

Chapter 3
Eli

"WHY DID I SAY I'D WEAR A TIE?" EVERETT ASKED as he worked his collar.

I snorted and looked over at my younger brother. "Because it's a wedding and its formal, and we were told by Roy we *had* to wear a tie. It's not my fault you borrowed Elijah's rather than buying one for yourself."

Everett sighed, worked his collar again. "I know I'm going to need to buy an actual suit that fits if we do this. It's also not my fault that I looked damn fine in my dress blues, but my shoulders outgrew my old suit. Hell, I'm going to be the CFO, damn it, I should look the part."

I held back a grin, knowing that Everett might

be growling slightly at the plan, but I knew he was in. Of all of my brothers, he was the most into it. That was Everett. Quiet sometimes, but determined.

"You're in then? CFO and everything? You've got the background and the degree for it."

Everett gave me a look, a single brow raised. "Of course, I'm in. I was in when you first mentioned it, even though it sounds insane."

I held back a laugh since I didn't want to draw too much attention to us. "I guess that would make me CEO. Though I don't want to think about being your boss."

Everett shook his head. "You've always been our boss. You're the big brother. The only one you couldn't order around is Eliza, but then again, none of us can order around our little sister."

That made my lips twitch, and I took a sip of the champagne the waiter had brought about. I wasn't a huge champagne fan, but it tasted good, and I felt like I needed the liquid courage to be here. It was odd to be somewhat crashing a wedding, though Roy said we could come as observers. We weren't going to eat or draw attention to ourselves, but it was good to watch what Roy and his team were doing. I knew there was a wedding planner around somewhere, one that Roy hired on since he didn't have one on staff. However, Roy was thinking about hiring someone permanently.

If the Wilders did go along with this insane plan, we'd be following Roy's footsteps to the letter.

"I don't know how to take that. Am I bossy?"

Everett grinned. "Yes. You're colossally bossy. It's what you do. Then again, you were the only officer among us."

I shrugged. "I got lucky with a scholarship and placement right out of high school, and things worked out for me. I was also in longer than any of you."

"And now we're all out, a bunch of NCOs without jobs."

"Local accounting jobs at the warehouses not doing it for you?" I teased.

"I hope that this works out because I'd rather you be my boss than anyone else. Yeah, you get annoying sometimes, but you're my brother. I wiped your brow after you threw up after too many drinks. I feel like that connects us."

I snorted. I couldn't help it. "You did that for East. He's your twin. Not for me. I'm a little too old for that."

There was a seven-year age gap between the twins and me, even more so between Elliott and me and Eliza. There were seven of us, and honestly, not too many years between us. I didn't know how my parents had done it, and never got a chance to ask before they died.

"Think we can do this?" I asked after a moment, looking at the party in front of us.

"Plan a wedding? No. Do everything else? Yes, I think we can."

I looked at him then, my eyes wide. "Just like that."

"Not just like that. You had notebooks and files on what it takes. And we're going to that workshop about inns and owning your own business."

"One where Roy promises it's not a timeshare scam." We both laughed at that before I continued. "We'll learn, and we've got the money to do it. I mean, I guess we could use the money for other things, but this is for our future, not just for a new car or new house."

Everett's lips twitch. "Considering most of us will end up living on the property if things work out well, it *is* a new house. And we've got decent cars. And there'll be enough after we buy the place to hopefully to get a new truck or two since we'll need it. For hauling."

"And because we live in Texas and need to fit in," I said with a laugh.

"And you know that Evan is going to thrive on the winery side."

I swallowed hard at Everett's words. "He will. If he lets himself."

"That's a big if. But, hell, he's the one who worked with the uncles for the longest. He's the main reason that we even had this opportunity. Not that we can let him know that."

I smiled despite myself. "You're right. We could figure things out but he's the glue. We each have a job. Each have a purpose. We work together. We wouldn't split up, take too much time away from each other like we've been doing for twenty years. Hell, I left the house to go pursue my own future when you guys were babies."

"I wasn't a baby. Sure, Eliza was, but I wasn't."

My lips twitched. "Close enough since you were like in puberty."

Everett sighed, looked over his shoulder. "Please, say that loudly for the people on the other side of the ball ballroom."

I looked around the vast room with the elevated ceilings and twinkling lights. "Our ballroom won't look like this."

"True, but ours would be in a renovated European-style farmhouse. The place is in good shape. It's like a fucking villa."

I snorted at the look of one of the guests at our cursing. "That was the goal for the original builders. They wanted to bring a little bit of Europe here with the architecture. So it is a villa of sorts in the middle of south Texas."

"Well, this is a little more upper-class farm."

I nodded. "We won't be competing for each other, even though we're a couple of hours away."

"Which is a good thing because we like Roy and need his help. We don't want to piss him off."

"Why don't you want to piss me off?" Roy asked as he walked over to us. Roy was a big man, mostly still muscle after all these years as a civilian, and he took care of himself. His hair was graying at the temples, and his full beard was white and gray now. He looked good, and he had been my friend for years. We had fought together, had been neighbors and even roommates for a bit in our early years. He was a couple of years older than me, so he got out before I did, but we had stayed in touch and, hopefully, he'd be able to help me figure out exactly what the hell I was going to do with the rest of my life.

"We were just thinking about taking your business," Everett said with a grin, and Roy just threw his head back and laughed, that big deep laugh that made everyone around us smile. Nobody glared at him. He was just the good guy who people got along with wherever he went.

Maybe that's why he was so good at this. I wasn't that guy. Whatever it was. Everett was. As was Elijah. And Elliot. East, Evan, and I were a little more on the asshole side of the family. But half of us being assholes, the other half being decent guys wasn't a bad mark.

"You're welcome to try, though. I think with the winery on your side and the brewery on mine, it's a good fit. We'll be able to send whoever can't fit into ours to each other. Working like a partnership, rather than adversaries."

The way that Roy said it, it seemed like a decree, and frankly, I agreed. "Sounds good to me. And honestly, it'll be nice having footsteps to follow in, even if we're trying to be our own bosses."

"I had footsteps too. The guy who owned this before I was a retired general."

"No shit?" I asked.

"Two star. Wanted something with his life a little bit different, and this was in the family. He sold it to me, and now you're buying from a former military man as well. It's all in the family, even though our family's a bit convoluted."

"Don't even begin on the whole convoluted family thing," Everett added with a grin.

Roy let out a big belly laugh that drew a few gazes our way. "There are seven of you, all starting with the same letter. What the hell was your mother thinking?"

I just smiled, used to the refrain. It had been worse when we'd all been active duty and went by Wilder. "We answered to numbers mostly. I was one."

"I don't remember my number. I think mom forgot it too." Everett said with a grin.

Roy leaned forward, laughing. "Well, you're a twin. I'm sure you and East switched off often just to annoy your parents."

"I can neither confirm nor deny."

Roy just grinned. "Well, you've had a look around. You saw the books and figured out what we do. What is it that you want?"

Everett looked to me, and I swallowed hard, rolling my shoulders back. "We want something that we can work together in. The place that we're looking at we would rename to Wilder Resorts. It has a good flow. It just needs some updating, but we can do that. Especially within the budget. We're already in talks, and they're not talking with anybody else right now for selling, so that's a good thing."

"Time is still on your side," Roy added.

"For sure. There are twenty cabins outside of the main building. The main building is a villa, with its own atrium and dining room and breakfast room and all that. The innkeeper can live there. And then within the cabins, we can designate some of those for the family like they did, so we can live on the property and not have to pay rent or mortgages on other places."

"That makes sense. We live in a house on the property. If you live in those cabins, are you going to cut into your bottom line?"

I shook my head. "No, this is what the other owners did before us with their teams. It makes sense. And while we all did training for other things when we were active duty, all of our degrees went towards what we thought we'd do as civilians versus what we did in the service. Oh, and we can take the cabins that need the most work for ourselves and work on them on our own."

Everett snorted. "Thanks for giving us the heaps to live in."

I raised a brow. "You've seen our land. There's nothing heap about it."

"That is true," Everett whispered.

"There's a pool, a sunning area with a shit-ton of tile that's perfect for photos according to the owner's daughter. And then, on the other side of the acreage, there's a winery with forested trails. There's a tasting room, barrel rooms, a large building for all the equipment. It's like its own business on the property."

Roy nodded along as we went over everything again. "And it's a lot of acres, more than I have. But then again, you need more land for the vines. Not that it's a huge heap of vines, but a respectable amount for good wines in moderation."

"It's a shit ton, but pricing right now is good, and I think we can make it work."

"I'm here if you need me, but it's a good opportunity. Yeah, it's different than what any of you guys did in the military, but hell, most of us were just handed an instruction packet once we joined, after we took a test to see what we were most suited for. Not that we knew what we were suited for, and then we went into that field. You can do that here."

I nodded. "We can. And hell, this might be nice. Something completely different."

"You're jumping into hospitality, think you can do it?"

I sighed, looked at my brother. "I think I want to."

"I don't think, I know." Everett grinned and then reached out and squeezed my other shoulder.

"Now to convince the others." That made me wince but Everett looked unfazed.

"They're not going to need convincing," Everett said with a tight nod. "They're already excited. Or at least as excited as they can be with their scowls."

"I sure do love your family," Roy said with a laugh. "And look, the garter toss is about to begin, go boys, go see if you're the next to get wed."

I blinked, looked at Roy. "I thought you said we needed to be casual observers."

"True, but there aren't as many single men here as there are single women, so go stand over there and fill the place so that way it's not three guys vying for a garter."

"Isn't that kind of archaic?" Everett asked, and I snorted.

"What he said. I'm not going to go catch a fucking garter."

"Go. Stand there. Don't hold out your hands.

Just stand there and look forward. Fill up the space."

"I don't understand you," I grumbled.

"You don't have to. You just have to do what I say."

"He did outrank you," Everett said with a grin, and I flipped my brother off before I lowered my head at Roy's glare, and walked over to where the dozen or so men were standing, hands in pockets, looking for all the world they would rather be anywhere else.

"They needed men for this, my ass," I grumbled, and Everett snorted.

"Hey, look on the bright side, the odds work in our favor now that we won't catch it, which is good. We have enough on our plate without getting married."

"My mom forced me over here, so I'm going to hide behind you," a man in his early twenties said as he smiled over at us. "If that's okay."

"Fuck no, you're not hiding behind me. I don't want the damn thing," I growled.

Everett just grinned, the asshole. "Nobody does, but here we are, at a place where love and happy ever after is the only thing that matters."

I shook my head and stood there, hands in

pockets as the bride sat down on a chair, and everybody started to cheer. Music began, and the groom went down on his knees, slid his hands up the bride's dress, and slowly, very slowly took her garter down.

"Well then, I feel like we're part of a peep show," Everett mumbled out of the side of his mouth, and I elbowed him to keep him quiet. He let out an oof, and when the groom stood up, swung the garter over his head, I held back a sigh. Apparently, we would have to get used to this, because a big part of the income were events and weddings on the property. I was going to have to start enjoying shit like this if this is what I wanted to do with the rest of my life.

Everybody started shouting, laughing, and I looked up as the garter was flung from the groom's hand and slapped me directly in the chest. On instinct, I reached out and gripped it and blinked.

"Fuck," Everett said with a laugh as everybody cheered.

"Better you than me," the younger man said before he rushed off to where his mom stood. The kid's mom glared at me, and I looked down at the frilly white thing and just shook my head.

"Well, shit," I grumbled.

"Oh, look at you, you're the next to be wed. I'm so proud," Everett teased as he wiped away a fake tear.

Everybody started congratulating me, and there were a few curious looks, probably wondering where the hell I had come from. I was supposed to be lowkey for this wedding, and here I was catching the fucking garter.

We moved out of the way as the bride came back, tossing bouquet in hand. "Okay single ladies, let's see who's going to get a ring on it!"

I held back a groan at the cheesy joke and watched as a few dozen women all lined up, jokingly ready to fight for the bouquet.

My gaze caught the eyes of one woman as she stood off to the side, earbud in her ear as she looked around at the others. This had to be the wedding planner, the woman that I had seen before and nearly swallowed my tongue over.

"You're drooling," Everett whispered.

"She's hot. Can't help it."

"And she's not for you. Remember? We said no dating."

"When did we say that?" I asked as I shook my head.

"You're gone, just like that, one look, and you're gone."

I didn't answer. Instead, I watched as the bride tossed the bouquet, but she sort of twisted her body as she did so, laughing and probably a little bit drunk. The bouquet flew over the heads of the rest of the party and slammed into the wedding planner's face. She caught the bouquet, her eyes wide, and looked beyond mortified.

"Oh my God, I love it!" the bride screamed. "I knew the tea leaves said this. I knew it! Now, where's our garter man. We have to see the dance!"

I met the gaze of the wedding planner, and then I looked down at my garter and then back up again.

"Well shit."

Chapter 4
Eli

I SHOULDN'T HAVE BEEN SURPRISED WHEN ROY'S hand pressed on my shoulder and practically pushed me towards the woman holding the bouquet.

"Dance! Dance! Dance!"

The crowd cheered, egging us on, and I found myself standing in front of the wedding planner, her soft blue suit nearly gray, and noticed that it was also a dress of some sort. She looked regal and yet like she wanted to blend with the background—something I should have been doing as well.

"This is not happening," she mumbled under her breath, and my eyes widened.

"Nice." I hadn't meant to say that aloud, but

damn, I was the only one who was supposed to not want to be there. Not her.

She blushed and looked up at me. "Sorry."

The bride moved forward, her eyes bright and a bit manic. "Dance! Come on, Alexis. It's my wedding. And I want you to dance, darling."

The wedding planner leaned forward, and I tried not to inhale her rich scent. "Phoenix, I need to help with the next part of the setup."

"You can do that after you dance." The bride put her smile towards me, all teeth and manic eyes. "And, hello stranger. I don't know who you are, so you're probably with my lovely groom. However, you are about to dance with one of my bestest friends. This is my wedding planner. Wedding planner, this is the stranger."

"Eli. My name is Eli."

The bride gave me another shark-tooth smile. "Good. Eli, darling. Now, dance. Dance for me, my pretties!" she said with a clap of her hands as her groom came forward, rolled his eyes, and pulled her back.

The groom grinned. "Just do what she says, and it'll all be over quick." He winked as he said it, then kissed his bride's neck, and she let out a little giggle. The two seemed in love, and like they were perfect for one another, even if the bride seemed a little high-strung. However, it was her wedding, so for all I knew, this was just an abnormality.

"Come on, let's just get this over with," the wedding planner mumbled under her breath as she slid her hand into mine.

"It'll be over before you know it," I replied with a grin as I put my hand on the small of her back. Her eyes widened, and I swallowed hard at the feel of her against me. She was all soft and curved, and it was hard for me to focus. Fuck, it was just hard for me in general. She was beautiful. Gorgeous, and she smelled like sin. Or maybe that was just floral perfume. I didn't know, but she was gorgeous. How was I supposed to focus when she was pressed up against me?

"Hopefully, the song will be over soon. I'm sorry. I don't mean to be a jerk, but I do have things to do for the wedding, and I'm not supposed to actually be around and in the spotlight like this."

I swallowed hard as the music turned into something softer, and we danced carefully.

"I should probably tell you then I shouldn't be in the spotlight either."

Her eyes narrowed even as her lips twitched. "Tell me I'm not dancing with a wedding crasher."

"Technically, I was invited. Just not by the wedding party."

She looked up at me, blinked. "You are with Roy then."

I frowned. "I don't know if *with Roy* is the right statement."

She laughed and it lit up her whole damn face. What the hell was with this connection? "You're here to watch Roy and to see what he does because you're thinking about buying something similar. To join the innkeepers and wedding venue circuit."

I couldn't stop staring at her mouth, so it took me a minute to catch up with her words. "I didn't realize he told you all that."

"Of course, Roy told me. We're about to have strangers at the wedding. I should have put it together beforehand, but I've been a little side-tracked. Busy day."

"It sure looks like it. The wedding looks fantastic, though."

"I hope so." She looked around, smiling softly. "We worked hard on it. And the bride and groom are beautiful together."

I looked over at them as they swayed from side to side, not dancing, just the two of them holding one another off the dance floor. It was just the two of us on the dance floor. Alone. With all eyes on us.

I held back a frown at the thought, even with the warmth of the woman in my arms. "I don't know if I like being the center of attention. I won't be once we run the place."

She smiled softly at me, her eyes filled with understanding. "No, you won't be. And neither one of us should be here in the limelight now."

I grinned. "I won't tell if you won't."

"I think the cat's out of the bag on that one," she whispered, her eyes dancing with laughter. She smelled so good and felt fucking amazing against me. I wanted her. Just like that, I wanted her.

There was a connection there, I could feel it, and from the way that she swayed into me, even though I knew she didn't want to because she was working, I felt like maybe she felt it too. Or maybe that's just what I wanted. What I was dreaming about and imagining.

"You're a wedding planner then. But you don't work for Roy full-time."

"He told you that?"

"Seems like Roy likes talking about everyone in his circles to each other," I said with a laugh.

"Seems like. And I own my own business. It

would be nice just to work for Roy, but Roy wasn't sure if he wanted a full-time wedding planner since he has an event planner on hand."

I nodded softly. "We're thinking along the lines of having both. Because my brother Elliot would be great at all the other planning that comes to the resort, and any minute details that would come about. However, wedding planning isn't something we've ever done before."

"And running an entire inn and business like this is?"

"You got me there, but I don't know if Elliot really wants to do that."

"So would you hire on a wedding planner ad hoc, or would you have one on full-time?"

"That's the discussion right now, and we're leaning towards full-time."

She grinned, and I couldn't help in joining her. "Sounds like you guys are planning well."

"If this weekend goes well, we sign on the dotted line on Monday."

Her eyes widened, even as my heart raced. I didn't know if it was the thought that we'd be spending a shit-ton of money on Monday or that smile on her face.

Damn it, I didn't have time for this or complications, and yet I wanted her.

There was something seriously fucking wrong with me.

"Well, I think Roy said this would be a couple of hours away, so not exactly in my jurisdiction as it were, but I know some people. I'll make sure you get my card afterward."

"I see, you just want to give me your number?" I asked, teasing. I surprised myself by even saying it since that wasn't normally like me, but she just smiled at me and shook her head.

"For work, buddy. I *am* working."

The song began to shift to something else as people came out onto the dance floor, joining us, and I almost hated the interruption. But the connection didn't snap. It didn't go away. It was still there.

"That's our cue. It was lovely meeting you, Eli. And I will get you my card." She paused. "For work."

"Whatever you say. The wedding is gorgeous."

"Thank you, and I hope you sign on that dotted line on Monday. I don't know. I just have a good feeling."

So did I, but I didn't say it. At least not then.

I followed her off the dance floor, ready to see if

she wanted a drink, even if she was working. I couldn't help it. Everett gave me a weird look, but I turned and kept my attention on the woman I couldn't keep my mind off.

That was when I noticed the man in the slick gray suit, fancy haircut, and wide smile on his face come up to her.

She stiffened for just a moment.

"Clint," she whispered as she pushed her honey-brown hair back from her face. Some of it had fallen from her bun and made her look far more disheveled than she was.

Clint. Well then. Either this guy was an ex, someone she didn't want to meet, or someone that was going to ruin any plans that I had.

"Baby. I talked it over with the bride, and well, you are amazing. I love you." He went down to one knee, and the bride started to squeal, clapped her hands as everybody started to murmur in hushed tones, either cheering or with wide eyes.

I looked at the man on one knee in front of the woman I swore I'd had a connection with, at her wide eyes, and held back a sigh.

Fuck.

I turned to see Everett there, his own eyes wide.

"You know what, let's do this. Wilder Resorts. We can do this. The six of us. We'll figure it out."

My brother cleared his throat. "I know we will. And what about the girl?"

I held back a snort as we made our way through the crowd, people cheering around us. "Clearly not for me. I don't need a woman. We all know what happens when we let our guard down.

"Yeah. We do."

And with that, I left the wedding alongside my brother. The two of us ready to meet with the other four and plan the rest of our lives. We had shit to do. Things that were all Wilder and just for us.

And I pushed all thoughts of a wedding planner, a bright smile, and a connection that clearly hadn't been real out of my mind.

Chapter 5
Alexis

I STOOD TRANSFIXED AS MY BOYFRIEND OF TWO years knelt in front of me in his Armani suit, and I just blinked. Mortification slid over me, embarrassment slamming into it.

"Clint," I whispered fiercely, wondering what the hell he could have been thinking. *This was someone else's wedding.*

Not only were public proposals tacky, but they were also the worst things in the history of all wedding planning. *You never proposed in public.* What if the person wanted to say no? What if things got weird? Because they were already really fucking weird.

I loved Clint. I truly did. I knew we were going to get married.

But how could he not know me well enough to understand that a public proposal at a wedding I was working at would not be a good idea? Why did he think that that would be a good idea?

"Baby. I love you. You plan all the weddings. You put everyone else's needs and happy ever afters in front of your own. Now, baby, it's time to plan your own happy ever after. To plan ours."

I just blinked at him, my mouth going dry. "Clint."

"I know you're looking at me like I've lost my damn mind. Maybe I have. But I love you. I've already talked to the bride and groom. You know I work with him."

"Oh. Right."

Why couldn't I say anything longer than a word or two? Why couldn't I focus or breathe? Why couldn't I do anything other than want to run away but unable to do so?

"I love you, Alexis. I want to spend the rest of my life with you. Here on the happiest days of two of my friends, they gave me permission to ask you to make me the happiest man on this earth." I looked over his shoulder sharply at the bride and groom as they held each other, tears flowing down the bride's cheeks. She gave me a thumbs-up and mimicked drinking tea, and I wanted to pass out. Over and away.

She had seen this in her tea leaves. Of course she had.

I looked to the right to see Emily rushing towards me, her mouth gaping open, her eyes wide.

I saw the look of *what the fuck* on her face, and it mirrored my own.

However, if I walked away, if I broke down and broke Clint's heart right here, I would be the bitch of all bitches. I would ruin this wedding and put a pall over everything. Nobody would ever want to hire me again. I would lose my job. Lose my sanity. I would lose everything.

This man, the love of my life, had proposed to me in the worst way possible for a wedding planner, but he seems so earnest about it.

I couldn't ruin this day for anyone.

I wanted this, I reminded myself. I wanted happiness.

Clint was mine. He was my forever.

We might as well start now and not ruin everything that I had worked towards along the way.

I lean down, and whispered, "Yes."

He beamed as he went to his feet and cheered, "She said yes!"

"Champagne for everybody!" The bride shouted out, and the room cheered, clapping each other on the back and laughing and taking photos. Clint cupped my face and kissed me softly.

"I knew you would love this. I knew this was perfect."

I looked at the man that I loved, at my fiancé, as he slid the ring onto my finger, a ring I didn't even notice because I couldn't breathe, and had to wonder if I had just made the biggest mistake of my life.

Alexis and Eli's romance is only beginning. Want to know what happens next? Start the Wilder Brothers with: One Way Back to Me!!

Acknowledgments

The Cage Family series has been on my mind for a few years and I knew it wasn't going to be easy. I was so grateful to my support crew in making this story work!

Brandi - you're my right hand. Or maybe my left? Or…well you know what you are. Thank you for keeping the inbox manageable and for being my rambling partner.

Tina and Emily - I'm forever grateful for our far too many signings. Our friendship has been a true highlight while working on this series and I'm honored to have you as my sounding board. (And yes, all the special things are coming!)

To Ann, Lauren, and the Crew at Milk & Cookies - Thank you. You took my love of spreadsheets and calendars and made it shine. I cannot wait to see what happens next!

Amy - thank you for listening to my panic and being such a fantastic editor! The Cages adore you!

To everyone who helped shape this book,

THANK YOU. This world might be scary and feel solitary, but I'm not alone because of you.

To you, my dear reader, thank you for being here. For always. And I cannot WAIT for you to meet the Wilders!

Also from Carrie Ann Ryan

The Montgomery Ink Legacy Series:

Book 1: Bittersweet Promises (Leif & Brooke)

Book 2: At First Meet (Nick & Lake)

Book 2.5: Happily Ever Never (May & Leo)

Book 3: Longtime Crush (Sebastian & Raven)

Book 4: Best Friend Temptation (Noah, Ford, and Greer)

Book 4.5: Happily Ever Maybe (Jennifer & Gus)

Book 5: Last First Kiss (Daisy & Hugh)

Book 6: His Second Chance (Kane & Phoebe)

Book 7: One Night with You (Kingston & Claire)

Book 8: Accidentally Forever (Crew & Aria)

Book 9: Last Chance Seduction (Lexington & Mercy)

The Wilder Brothers Series:

Book 1: One Way Back to Me (Eli & Alexis)

Book 2: Always the One for Me (Evan & Kendall)

Book 3: The Path to You (Everett & Bethany)

Book 4: Coming Home for Us (Elijah & Maddie)

Book 5: Stay Here With Me (East & Lark)

Book 6: Finding the Road to Us (Elliot, Trace, and Sidney)

Book 7: Moments for You (Ridge & Aurora)

Book 7.5: A Wilder Wedding (Amos & Naomi)

Book 8: Forever For Us (Wyatt & Ava)

Book 9: Pieces of Me (Gabriel & Briar)

Book 10: Endlessly Yours (Brooks & Rory)

The Cage Family

Book 1: The Forever Rule (Aston & Blakely)

Book 2: An Unexpected Everything (Isabella & Weston)

Book 3: If You Were Mine (Dorian & Harper)

The First Time Series:

Book 1: Good Time Boyfriend (Heath & Devney)

Book 2: Last Minute Fiancé (Luca & Addison)

Book 3: Second Chance Husband (August & Paisley)

The Montgomery Ink: Fort Collins Series:

Book 1: Inked Persuasion (Jacob & Annabelle)

Book 2: Inked Obsession (Beckett & Eliza)

Book 3: Inked Devotion (Benjamin & Brenna)

Book 3.5: Nothing But Ink (Clay & Riggs)

Book 4: Inked Craving (Lee & Paige)

Book 5: Inked Temptation (Archer & Killian)

The Montgomery Ink: Boulder Series:

Book 1: Wrapped in Ink (Liam & Arden)

Book 2: Sated in Ink (Ethan, Lincoln, and Holland)

Book 3: Embraced in Ink (Bristol & Marcus)

Book 3: Moments in Ink (Zia & Meredith)

Book 4: Seduced in Ink (Aaron & Madison)

Book 4.5: Captured in Ink (Julia, Ronin, & Kincaid)

Book 4.7: Inked Fantasy (Secret ??)

Book 4.8: A Very Montgomery Christmas (The Entire Boulder Family)

Montgomery Ink: Colorado Springs

Book 1: Fallen Ink (Adrienne & Mace)

Book 2: Restless Ink (Thea & Dimitri)

Book 2.5: Ashes to Ink (Abby & Ryan)

Book 3: Jagged Ink (Roxie & Carter)

Book 3.5: Ink by Numbers (Landon & Kaylee)

Montgomery Ink Denver:

Book 0.5: Ink Inspired (Shep & Shea)

Book 0.6: Ink Reunited (Sassy, Rare, and Ian)

Book 1: Delicate Ink (Austin & Sierra)

Book 1.5: Forever Ink (Callie & Morgan)

Book 2: Tempting Boundaries (Decker and Miranda)

Book 3: Harder than Words (Meghan & Luc)

Book 3.5: Finally Found You (Mason & Presley)

Book 4: Written in Ink (Griffin & Autumn)

Book 4.5: Hidden Ink (Hailey & Sloane)

Book 5: Ink Enduring (Maya, Jake, and Border)

Book 6: Ink Exposed (Alex & Tabby)

Book 6.5: Adoring Ink (Holly & Brody)

Book 6.6: Love, Honor, & Ink (Arianna & Harper)

Book 7: Inked Expressions (Storm & Everly)

Book 7.3: Dropout (Grayson & Kate)

Book 7.5: <u>Executive Ink</u> (Jax & Ashlynn)

Book 8: <u>Inked Memories</u> (Wes & Jillian)

Book 8.5: <u>Inked Nights</u> (Derek & Olivia)

Book 8.7: <u>Second Chance Ink</u> (Brandon & Lauren)

Book 8.5: Montgomery Midnight Kisses (Alex & Tabby Bonus(

Bonus: Inked Kingdom (Stone & Sarina)

The On My Own Series:

Book 0.5: My First Glance

Book 1: My One Night (Dillon & Elise)

Book 2: My Rebound (Pacey & Mackenzie)

Book 3: My Next Play (Miles & Nessa)

Book 4: My Bad Decisions (Tanner & Natalie)

The Promise Me Series:

Book 1: Forever Only Once (Cross & Hazel)

Book 2: From That Moment (Prior & Paris)

Book 3: Far From Destined (Macon & Dakota)

Book 4: From Our First (Nate & Myra)

The Less Than Series:

Book 1: Breathless With Her (Devin & Erin)

Book 2: Reckless With You (Tucker & Amelia)

Book 3: Shameless With Him (Caleb & Zoey)

The Fractured Connections Series:

Book 1: Breaking Without You (Cameron & Violet)

Book 2: Shouldn't Have You (Brendon & Harmony)

Book 3: Falling With You (Aiden & Sienna)

Book 4: Taken With You (Beckham & Meadow)

The Whiskey and Lies Series:

Book 1: <u>Whiskey Secrets</u> (Dare & Kenzie)

Book 2: <u>Whiskey Reveals</u> (Fox & Melody)

Book 3: <u>Whiskey Undone</u> (Loch & Ainsley)

The Gallagher Brothers Series:

Book 1: <u>Love Restored</u> (Graham & Blake)

Book 2: <u>Passion Restored</u> (Owen & Liz)

Book 3: <u>Hope Restored</u> (Murphy & Tessa)

The Ravenwood Coven Series:

Book 1: Dawn Unearthed

Book 2: Dusk Unveiled

Book 3: Evernight Unleashed

The Aspen Pack Series:

Book 1: Etched in Honor

Book 2: Hunted in Darkness

Book 6: <u>Hidden Destiny</u>

Book 6.5: <u>A Beta's Haven</u>

Book 7: <u>Fighting Fate</u>

Book 7.5: <u>Loving the Omega</u>

Book 7.7: <u>The Hunted Heart</u>

Book 8: <u>Wicked Wolf</u>

The Elements of Five Series:

Book 1: From Breath and Ruin

Book 2: From Flame and Ash

Book 3: From Spirit and Binding

Book 4: From Shadow and Silence

Dante's Circle Series:

Book 1: <u>Dust of My Wings</u>

Book 2: <u>Her Warriors' Three Wishes</u>

Book 3: <u>An Unlucky Moon</u>

Book 3.5: <u>His Choice</u>

Book 4: <u>Tangled Innocence</u>

Book 5: <u>Fierce Enchantment</u>

Book 6: <u>An Immortal's Song</u>

Book 7: <u>Prowled Darkness</u>

Book 8: Dante's Circle Reborn

Holiday, Montana Series:

Book 1: <u>Charmed Spirits</u>

Book 2: <u>Santa's Executive</u>

Book 3: <u>Finding Abigail</u>

Book 4: <u>Her Lucky Love</u>

Book 5: Dreams of Ivory

The Branded Pack Series:

(Written with Alexandra Ivy)

Book 1: <u>Stolen and Forgiven</u>

Book 2: <u>Abandoned and Unseen</u>

Book 3: <u>Buried and Shadowed</u>

About the Author

Carrie Ann Ryan is the New York Times and USA Today bestselling author of contemporary, paranormal, and young adult romance. Her works include the Montgomery Ink, Redwood Pack, Fractured Connections, and Elements of Five series, which have sold over 3.0 million books worldwide. She started writing while in graduate school for her advanced degree in chemistry and hasn't stopped since. Carrie Ann has written over seventy-five novels and novellas with more in the works. When she's not losing herself in her emotional and action-packed worlds, she's reading as much as she can while wrangling her clowder of cats who have more followers than she does.

www.CarrieAnnRyan.com